Darby

Love is strong.

xo
ashleypullo

Darby

A New Amsterdam novel by

ashley pullo

Print & eBook formatting by Erika Q. Stokes

Cover art by Molly Van Roekel

Proofreading by Marla Esposito

Paperback cover design by Nick Fantini

"The world breaks everyone, and afterward, some are strong at the broken pieces."

~ Ernest Hemingway

To the humans of New York and the true heroes of the streets, NYC's Strongest, the DSNY.

In the summer of 2010, photographer Brandon Stanton began an ambitious project – to single-handedly create a photographic census of New York City. The photos he took and the accompanying interviews became the blog Humans of New York. (St. Martin's, 2015).

Prologue

In his defense, the man wearing the expensive plum blossom aftershave had it coming.

As the City prepares for an impending snow storm, and the temperature plummets to a single digit, New Yorkers stock their refrigerators and liquor cabinets, and then pray that a potential power outage won't interfere with their Netflix streaming.

Every January, without fail, the island of Manhattan transforms into a winter wonderland ... sledding in Central Park, snowball fights on narrow streets, and the beautiful stillness of falling snow ... and, um ... *Oh, fuck it*! New York winters suck. Brown sludge, salty sidewalks, and gaping potholes ... staying in, digging out, and prepping for more ... dry hands, cracked lips, and stale conversation. It's the most annoying six to twelve weeks of the year for snow-hating urban dwellers.

But the truth is, although New Yorkers love to complain, they also strive to maintain a sense of complacency in a changing world.

And so it's the resiliency of Lower Manhattan that reigns superior; a place where people can stand with reverence in the wake of disasters to fight for the revival of humanity. Hurricanes, fires, Scorsese films, floods, terrorism, and blizzards, cannot deter the ideology of the strong and determined. Serving as the foundation of this great city, and the gathering place for a fortified population for centuries, Battery Park is the shield of the City – the prow of New Amsterdam.

And this is where the story continues . . .

Double-parking his Lexus GS F outside the Whole Foods on Greenwich Street, Paul Holbrook locks his doors and then rushes inside the grocery store. Passing on the organic tangerines, he heads straight toward the legume section to fill his basket with green beans. Tossing in a few bags of baby carrots, he then proceeds to the seafood department. Rudely cutting the short line, Paul taps his fingers on the glass display and asks, "Salmon steaks?"

Weighing a generous helping of sea scallops, the seafood employee retorts, "Yeah, over there. Pre-packaged."

"Frozen?"

"No, man, never frozen," he replies with a scowl. "But if you wait in line like everyone else, I could show you."

Clicking his tongue and arrogantly nodding his head, Paul grabs a lemon from a tiered basket and says, "I think I can handle it."

Somewhat satisfied with the selection of salmon steaks in the refrigerated display case, he takes two large packages and drops them in his basket. It wasn't his idea to make dinner for his ex-fiancée, and in fact, he's not interested in rekindling the relationship with Kelly, but winter in the City is lonely, and sex with Kelly is a sure thing.

Making one last stop in the wine section, he grabs a bottle of Chardonnay just as an attractive brunette reaches for the same label. Paul runs his eyes over her tight body and offers a line of seduction. "We have great taste."

Glancing at him while arching a thin brow, she replies, "Yes, you *and* my husband have great taste." She sets the bottle in her shopping cart and hurries off toward the bakery.

"You're not my type anyway," he mutters with a smirk.

Paul carries his basket to the *twelve items or less* register, joins the line, and then impatiently taps his foot. Counting the items of the man in front of him, he blurts, "You have sixteen items."

Placing his basket on the belt and intentionally removing each item one by one, the man replies, "Are you in a hurry?"

"Yeah, I am," he grunts.

"Well, that sucks for you, huh?"

Holding back his rage, Paul bites the inside of his cheek and clenches his fists. The pimply young cashier, aware of the impending situation, quickly scans and bags the sixteen grocery items while Paul dramatically unloads his own basket.

"Have a great night," the man calls over his shoulder with a smug grin.

"Fuck you, asshole," Paul huffs.

After paying for his groceries and snarling at the other customers when he takes a few extra paper bags, he hurries back to his illegally parked car on Greenwich Street. Digging the car keys out from his coat pocket, he stops at the curb to watch as a yellow cab brushes the driver's side of his eighty thousand dollar gray sedan. "Oh, you just did not! What the fuck?" he yells.

Darting to the street to stop the cab, Paul reaches inside his grocery bag and throws the first thing he finds – a package of expensive, wild-caught salmon. After a loud thud, the cab screeches to halt, nearly causing an accident on the congested, unplowed street.

The cab driver, mid-thirties and angry as hell, jumps out of his car to study the slimy package sliding down his back window. "What's wrong with you?" he shouts, peeling the salmon steak off the trunk. "Is this fish?"

"You hit my car, asshole."

"Oh, this car? The one that's parked illegally?" the cabbie asks, revealing a British accent.

Paul drops his grocery bag to the ground and lunges toward the cab driver. Standing at least a foot taller, and with veins protruding from his forehead, he pokes the cabbie's chest with his index finger and snarls between gritted teeth. "You hit my fucking car. A car that costs more than your entire village of camels, you fucking turban head."

Narrowing his eyes and puffing his chest, the cab driver calmly replies, "Do you see a fucking turban on my head? You stupid, white, racist motherfucker."

"Pakistani piece of shit – I'm going to kick your ass." Paul shoves the cab driver against the trunk of the taxi and grabs the collar of his leather jacket.

"I'm from London, dipshit," the cab driver shouts, just as an NYPD patrol car rolls up next to them.

The sirens whoop and flash, and then a young, African American officer steps out of the car. His partner, an even younger, Hispanic officer remains inside explaining the situation to dispatch.

"I'm going to need you to step back," the officer demands, grabbing Paul's arm, twisting it behind his waist, and then pulling him away from the taxi driver.

"He threw a fish at my cab, and then attacked me! I'd like to report a hate crime."

"Brother, you got it all wrong," whines Paul. "That asshole hit *my* car and threatened me."

"Do *not* call me brother," orders the officer. "And you," he directs his attention to the cab driver, "Shut up."

Glancing back over his shoulder as he tightens his grip around Paul's arm, the officer says, "What do you think, Mendez? Should we haul 'em in?"

Joining his partner, Officer Mendez crosses his arms and scowls. "It's up to you Dobson. We'll have to get the tow trucks down here before the snow storm."

"Oh, come on!" shouts Paul. "Arrest me for what exactly?"

"Disorderly conduct requires the least amount of paperwork on my part," replies Officer Dobson, taking a whiff of Paul's potent cologne. "Public intoxication is an easy one as well. Or, we can act like civilized men and exchange insurance information. It's up to you."

"Fine by me," the cab driver says, raising his hands to surrender.

"Whatever," Paul mutters.

"All right then. Mendez, you handle the cab, I'll take the Lexus." Dobson releases Paul's arm, allowing him to examine the yellow scratch on the side panel of his car. "I need your license and registration, sir."

"Here," Paul replies, removing the IDs from his wallet and chucking them at Dobson.

"Watch yourself," demands Dobson. While filling out the incident report on a handheld device, he checks the posted parking signs and asks, "So you were just parked here for a few minutes and the cab swiped your door?"

"Yeah," Paul answers, running his finger over the ding in his side mirror. "He would have left, too. They're all the same."

"They?"

Staring the officer directly in the eyes, he snaps, "Illegal, non-taxpaying, immigrants who dirty our streets."

Narrowing his eyes and peering down at Paul, Dobson says, "Right. You and I have to stick together, huh?"

Sensing the sarcasm, Paul whines, "Are we almost done here?"

"You have a fine piece of expensive machinery. Too bad you doubled-parked." Dobson smirks, printing an e-ticket from his handheld device. "You'll need to pay this before the court date."

"Yeah, yeah," Paul replies, crumpling the ticket and stashing it in his pocket.

"What about the fish he threw at my cab?" the taxi driver shouts.

Rolling his eyes, Officer Mendez says, "I think my partner told you to shut up."

As Paul removes his phone to take photos of the scratch, a sanitation officer knocks on the roof of his Lexus. "Hey, man, is that your bag of groceries and broken wine bottle?" he asks, pointing to the Whole Foods bag and shattered glass near a sidewalk trashcan.

"Yeah, that's mine. So?"

"And what's your name?" the sanitation officer asks, peering inside the window of the Lexus. "Damn, is that custom red leather?"

Reading from Paul's license, Officer Dobson interjects, "His name is Paul Holbrook, and he's a non-organ donor."

"You need to have a little more respect for our city, man." The sanitation officer hands Paul another e-ticket. "Littering and improper disposal of broken glass is reprehensible, and quite frankly, the selfish act of a real douchebag."

Cackling like a mad man, Paul wads the ticket into a ball. "You must be fucking kidding me!" He tosses it on the ground and steps on it, burying it under the layers of slush and grime left from the melting snow.

"Wrong move, Paul." Speaking into the radio clipped to his shoulder, Mendez happily reports, "This is Officer Mendez again. We're going to need that police impound truck at Greenwich and Warren."

In a swift tackle, Officer Dobson cuffs Paul's hands behind his back and leads him to the backseat of his patrol car. As he forces Paul's head down and shoves him in the backseat, Dobson gets another whiff of the expensive plum blossom aftershave. Laughing, he asks, "Paul, brother, what's up with your fruity perfume?"

But in Dobson's defense, the racist motherfucker had it coming.

"Living alone in a city with eight million people is a luxury – I listen to jazz, watch television, order takeout for one, drink exceptional whisky, and sleep with whomever I want, whenever I want. But it's the alone part that eventually manifests into loneliness, and without warning, I'm a ghost."

Chapter One

"I'm so close. So, so, so-oh-oh . . ." A sweaty lock of red hair sticks to her mouth, as beads of perspiration trickle down her naked back, but she has no intention of slowing down. "Faster. Ha-huh-harder," she orders, knowing she will either orgasm or black out – both sensations equally satisfying on a winter night.

Her late-night guest moans . . . deep and wild, craving immediacy, and begging to release. "It's so fucking hot in here," he mutters, shifting his muscular thighs beneath her writhing body.

She laughs.

He smiles.

She grinds as he thrusts – a shared rhythm synced to the clicking of the radiator.

Tightening her grasp around his cock, and digging her nails into his shoulders, she bites her lip and surrenders. *God bless, Kegels,* she thinks.

Giving her full control, he sensually kisses the stretch of skin beneath her breast, and then latches on to the soft flesh of her nipple. He squeezes her hips with his hands while sliding to the edge of the ripped velvet chair to achieve optimum penetration.

Eyes closed, she whimpers, "I'm coming." She presses her hands against his sweaty chest and rides out the last second of a surging orgasm.

"Oh, fuck. Me too," he pants.

Slowly opening her eyes to watch her partner's climatic release, she moans. "That was hot, Anthony."

"Uncomfortably hot, Darby." Wiping his brow with his forearm, Anthony asks, "What's wrong with your heater? I almost passed out."

Darby climbs off Anthony's lap and stands, her languid body numb and sore. She slaps the rusty frame of the steam radiator and says, "McToasty lost his little valve thingy last winter when I threw a boot at him." She grabs a T-shirt from the floor – bright, neon-green with the Department of Sanitation emblem ironed across the chest. "I tried to replace it with a bicycle tire valve, but that just pissed him off."

Narrowing his eyes and shaking his head, Anthony snorts. "McToasty?"

"Yeah, he's Scottish, like me." Darby smiles as she pulls the green cotton over her head, flattening her strawberry curls. The shirt swallows her petite frame, falling to the top of her bony knees, and even in the dimly-lit corner of her apartment, she glows. "Do you want a drink?" she asks, passing Anthony a small wastebasket overflowing with garbage.

He drops his condom in the trashcan and then peels his sweaty ass away from the velvet chair, cupping his penis in his large hand as he stands. "I'll have whatever you're having." Anthony retrieves his boxers from the cluttered coffee table and heads toward the tiny bathroom. "Do you mind if I take a cold shower?"

Watching the snow accumulate on the fire escape outside her only window, Darby replies, "Knock yourself out, but McSudsy is a fickle bitch. You have to *really* crank her handle while saying a prayer to the old gods and the new, and then belt a *Cure* song."

"Got it." Anthony closes the bathroom door behind him and starts the shower. "Do you give every inanimate object a Scottish name?" he shouts over the creaking noise of the pipes.

Darby rubs her eyes, and then pulls her hair into a high ponytail. "Only the ones that like it." Smiling, she moves to the tiny kitchenette and takes two coffee mugs from an open shelf. She grabs a bottle of whisky from the counter and pours herself a generous splash, listening to Anthony's deep baritone belt "Boys Don't Cry." Tightening her lips and slapping the counter, Darby throws back the whisky in a single gulp. As she shakes off the burning sensation and refills her mug, an unfamiliar beeping sound echoes beneath Anthony's pile of clothes.

She takes a sip from the mug and then sets it on the counter. *Slow down,* she nags.

After the second round of beeps, she patters toward the bathroom and waits for the shower to stop. "Anthony?" Darby pushes the door open to the bathroom, causing him to knock things off the shelf above the toilet.

"What the hell, woman?" he teases, stepping out of the shower. "Pass me McTowel."

Taking her time to reach for a towel, she studies every inch of his naked, wet body. "Sorry," she apologizes with a wink.

Anthony wraps the towel around his waist and returns a playful grin. "And next time, we go to my place."

Darby runs her hand over his amazing, fuzzy chest, fantasizing about future hypotheticals, but ultimately choosing to ignore his last comment. "Do you have to go to work?"

"Yeah, unfortunately." Anthony drops the wet towel on the floor and grabs his boxer briefs. "Have you ever tried to catch a train to Queens during a snowstorm?"

"Queens? Never." Darby fakes disgust as she walks back to the main room. "Is your garbage route in Queens?"

"Nah. But I was planning to go home before my shift." He follows behind her, picking up his wet towel and search for a hook.

"I'm sorry, Anthony."

Anthony grins. "For what?"

Answering him in the best way she knows how, Darby points to the window. "The weather sucks." *And I'm a miserable person who deserves to be alone.*

He takes her hand and leads her to the far corner of the apartment. Drawing a smiley face with his finger on the cold pane of glass, he says, "But you get to draw on windows!"

"I, uh . . ." The walls of her throat close. "I think your phone's beeping," she rasps.

Anthony looks back at the sofa and frowns. "Dammit." He lets go of her hand and hurries to the pile of clothes left on the floor. Removing his phone from the pocket of his jeans, he checks the NYC alerts and messages. "Salting at three," he mutters, pulling on his pants.

Meanwhile, Darby disappears to the kitchenette to grab the coffee mugs of whisky from the counter and a cereal box stashed above the refrigerator. "Then we have a little time."

Waggling his brows, he replies, "Time for what exactly?" Anthony takes the Cap'n Crunch from under her hand and plops down on the couch. "C'mere, Shortcake."

Cuddling next to his freshly showered chest, Darby hands him a mug of whisky.

"This isn't water, huh?"

"I drink whisky when I'm cold."

"It's like eighty degrees in here." He sets the mug on the coffee table and opens the box of cereal. "You know, Crunch isn't really a captain."

"What?"

"Yeah, he's a fraud."

"But it's just cereal."

"True, but he's representing the *S.S. Guppy*."

"I don't get it."

Pointing to the raised arm salute of Horatio Crunch, Anthony explains, "You see the stripes on his sleeve?"

"Yeah?"

"He only has three stripes – which makes him a commander. A captain in the Navy sports four stripes."

"Yeah, but Commander Crunch sounds like a video game." Squeezing his thigh gently, she asks, "Were you in the Navy?"

"Nah," he replies, shoving a handful of crunchy cereal in his mouth. "I thought about joining the Marines after college, but my cousin Joey talked me into taking a job with sanitation."

"You went to college?"

"Don't act so surprised, Darby!" He playfully nudges her away from his arm and says, "You think I'm a *stunad,* don't you?"

"What's a *stunad?*" She shakes her head.

"It's like Queens Italian for *stonato.*"

"Stonato?"

"Dumbfuck." With hooded eyes and a curled lip, Anthony imitates the gravelly voice of a Hollywood mobster. "My cousin Gino is a real *stunad.* The *goombah* quit his union job to move to Vegas with all the other *boombots. Capish?*"

Laughing, Darby adds, *"Eh, yo, bada bing, bada bing!"*

"Vattene!" he jokes, as he plants his sugar-coated lips on her forehead.

"Hey, that's not a real kiss!" she whines, her nose pressed against his stubbly jaw.

Wrapping the end of her ponytail around his finger, Anthony quietly replies, "I can't kiss you yet, Darby."

"What does that mean?" She snaps her head back and frowns. "We had sex on that chair like ten minutes ago!"

Sighing, Anthony tugs on her ponytail and pulls her back into his arms. "Sex on a chair is non-emotional physical compliancy – we both wanted that." He pauses, stroking her back and nuzzling his chin against her hair. "I'll kiss you when you want more than sex on a chair. I promise."

I do want more, she thinks.

But Darby doesn't say anything.

Instead, wrapped in each other's arms, Darby and Anthony watch as the snow flurries cover the window. Everything is quiet and still – as if this precise moment is being recreated inside a shoebox diorama for others to view.

And then Anthony's phone beeps. "Shit. I don't wanna to go to work," he grumbles.

"Then don't," she whispers.

"But who will plow the snow?" Reluctantly standing from the couch, Anthony pulls Darby up and kisses her hand. "I need my shirt, Shortcake." Slowly lifting the T-shirt over her head, he buries his mouth along the curve of her neck.

"You have me naked in your arms and yet you're leaving."

Grabbing a chenille throw from the sofa, Anthony wraps it around her tiny frame and bites his lip. "You naughty tease."

"Part of my charm." She winks. "But you should go before the storm hits."

"Yeah, if we lose power, my job becomes a whole lot harder," he huffs.

"Shit! I need to charge my phone." Darby picks up the end of her blanket and hurries to her desk.

Fishing for his Timberland boots under the coffee table, Anthony sits on the couch and puts on his T-shirt. He finds his flannel shirt tucked between the seat cushions, and his coat draped over a plastic cactus. Pulling on his wool socks and lacing his boots, Anthony says, "I'd really like to see you again." He stands from the couch and zips his coat. "What's Tuesday like for you?"

Darby ignores his question, distracting herself with the knotted cords to her laptop and phone chargers.

Stepping over dirty laundry to join her at the desk, he places his hands on her bare shoulders and whispers, "Darby?"

"This Tuesday?" Thinking fast, she opens the desk drawer and removes a discarded gum wrapper and a chewed pen. She spins around to face him and instructs, "Here – write your number on this."

Shocked by her odd request, Anthony takes the small paper and the pen and waits for an explanation. "A gum wrapper?"

"Um, yeah?" She shrugs her shoulders.

"I'm not sure if you know this, but iPhones can store thousands of contacts," he kids.

Lowering her head, she recites her go-to response. "Look, I'm not really into dating. But we could grab a drink sometime and maybe—"

"You mean you don't date men like me," Anthony interrupts.

"What? No, I, uh . . . it's me. I like being single I guess."

"You're lying." He lifts her chin and stares into her eyes. "Blue, green – who are you?"

She flinches.

"But, hey, I get it." Anthony scribbles something on the white side of the wrapper and then wads it into a tiny ball. "We're just single adults trying to have some fun until the weather's nice or someone better comes along." He fakes a smile and then flicks the shiny foil across the room, watching it as it disappears near the stacks of paperbacks and records. "Take care of yourself, Darby."

"Anthony," she pleads, following him to the door.

"Yeah?"

Tightening the blanket around her body, she mutters, "Um, be careful out there."

Anthony nods with a thin smile and then shuts the door behind him.

Angry and confused, Darby latches the chain and deadbolts the door. Kicking a pair of snow boots out of the way, she hurries to the far corner of her studio apartment to search for the gum wrapper. She drops the blanket and falls to her knees, scraping a shin and stubbing a pinky toe.

And it's there – kneeling in the nude beneath her only window, alone and vulnerable, Darby Wallace begins to sob.

Chapter Two

Eight hours earlier . . .

Applying red lip gloss in the lobby bathroom of the NYC Marriott, Darby checks her appearance in the mirror and blots her mouth. She adjusts her bra beneath her sheer sweater, and then runs her fingers through her wavy, strawberry-blond hair. As she returns the lip gloss to her clutch, her phone vibrates with a text from her older brother. Leaning against the counter, she reads the text aloud – because she's alone in a marble bathroom and digs the way her raspy voice echoes through the space. In her best impression of Grant Dougal Wallace, she says—

Grant: Camille wants to know if you'd like to come over for dinner.

Bleh, she thinks.

Darby: What are you having?

Grant: Beet Wellington.

Darby: Beef?

Grant: B E E T

Darby: I'm beginning to think you left your balls in Palo Alto.

She snorts, amused by her go-to dig about Grant's West Coast softness after returning to New York.

Grant: Hilarious. Dinner?

Darby: Raincheck? I'm walking into the Singles in the City event at the Marriott.

Grant: Whose idea was that?

Darby: Yours, fucker.

Grant: Oh, right. The Gotham article.

Darby: With just the right amount of alcohol consumption, I will either write a humorous piece mocking the dating rituals of singles in NYC, or . . . fall in love.

Grant: I look forward to the humorous piece.

Darby: You know that's right!

Exiting the bathroom, Darby surveys the lobby, hoping to find a rich bachelor without stepping foot into the singles mixer. Eyeing the only man in her visual perimeter, Darby smiles at the concierge at the check-in desk. He nods with a polite grin, and then picks up the telephone to make a call. Shrugging him off, she turns on her heels and heads the other direction toward the coat check.

Handing over her long, wool coat to the counter girl, Darby takes the numbered ticket and shoves it in the pocket of her tight jeans. As she walks toward the entrance of the Houston Ballroom, she's greeted by an attractive couple in their twenties, presumably the hosts, and definitely paid models.

Greeting Darby with a plastic smile, the man with slick hair and expensive suit nudges his co-host. "Hello."

"Hi," Darby replies, trying to decide what he's all about.

He looks her over as well, taking in her black clothing and contrasting pale skin. "Are you attending the social event this evening?"

"Single in the City? Yes, I am." Darby removes her phone from her clutch and opens a text with a QR code. "I registered online yesterday."

The female half of the couple picks up an iPad and scans the ticket. Reading from the screen, she announces, "Darby Wallace, Gotham Online, thirty years old, Holly Golightly." Snapping a blue wristband around Darby's tiny wrist, she explains, "The blue band denotes your age bracket, and your character name is printed on this side."

Staring at the name on her wristband, Darby mumbles, "Holly Golightly – the lonely slob who socializes with wealthy men in exchange for money. You have me pegged."

"Audrey Hepburn was an escort?"

"Um, no . . . in Capote's novella, Holly Golightly is a high-end call girl, but the movie romanticizes the original plot."

The woman shakes her head and places her hands on her narrow hips. "I don't follow."

"Never mind," huffs Darby.

"In order to break the ice, every guest is assigned a literary character that matches their personality traits – the test you completed when you registered for the event?" the man explains in a smug tone.

"I vaguely remember a personality test. But I do remember the promise of top-shelf liquor!" Darby chuckles, and then plays if off by clearing her throat.

After an awkward pause, the woman instructs, "Since you're a Holly Golightly from *Breakfast at Tiffany's*, you should avoid the Stanley Kowalskis and Patrick Batemans."

Mouth dropped, Darby whispers, "Wait, there are actually men in that ballroom with a personality match to *American Psycho*?"

"Oh, yeah! Probably our largest group. Mostly businessmen

with insatiable appetites for debauchery," the man replies, shaking his blue wristband with the name Patrick Bateman printed on the side.

Darby scrunches her nose and fakes a smile. "Cool. And about that open bar?"

Answering Darby's question like a trained flight attendant, the woman motions to the ballroom with two fingers. "Yes, through the double doors and to the left."

"Excellent," mutters Darby, darting toward the entrance.

She pushes open the door, carefully covering the band on her wrist while surveying the room. Most of the men are dressed in suits, but the women are a smorgasbord of stereotypes – skanks in short dresses, professionals in pantsuits, hipsters in vintage T-shirts, and virgins in fuzzy cashmere sweaters. Unimpressed by her prospects, and disappointed by the female representation, she heads toward the crescent-shaped bar to enjoy some liquid company.

A bartender, short and stocky, places a small napkin in front of Darby. "Would you like a drink?"

Eyeing the rows of bottles illuminated by neon lights, Darby spots her favorite Scotch whisky, Glendronach. It's smooth and buttery and perfect on its own, but she's in public, and people are watching, so she'll have to commit the biggest sin for a Scot – tarnish the peaty toffee flavor with soda. "I'll have the Glendronach fifteen year revival with a splash of ginger ale and um," she looks around, scowling at all the pretty single girls with vodka martinis, "and um, ice, I guess."

"Got it," he replies with a nod.

As the bartender prepares her drink, Darby studies the ballroom while typing a few notes on her phone.

Lounge vibe.

Mostly blue wristbands. Thirty-somethings or lying bastards.

100+ ppl.

Dumb hosts.

How many people here are paid models?

Is this a straight mixer only? Gays are always more fun.

$50/ticket is a scam.

But Glendronach is worth all the money!

"Cell phones are frowned upon," a deep voice warns, joining Darby at the bar.

Looking up from her phone, and tilting her head, she replies, "Oh, I'm not here to actually talk to anyone."

Amused by her candor, he smirks. "Well, damn. Now I *really* want to talk to you."

The bartender returns with Darby's drink and then turns to the man with the deep voice. "Can I get you something?"

"Gin and tonic, please."

Sipping casually from her dainty straw, Darby takes in the man's ruggedly handsome profile, watching as he analyzes every detail of the ballroom. His suit is charcoal, and his shirt is the color of ash, but his kind face and green eyes emit a sexy energy far removed from the colorless emotions of winter-gray. "Have you been to a lot of these?" she asks, using her sultry, redheaded vixen voice.

He glances at her and then looks straight ahead. "Nope, my very first one."

"Your gin and tonic," the bartender says, sliding the drink in the man's direction.

He turns around and picks up the glass, revealing an expensive watch and a blue wristband with the name Nick Carraway. "Have a great time," he politely says, clanking his glass against Darby's, and then arrogantly walking away.

Intrigued by his mysterious demeanor, Darby grabs her clutch from the bar and follows behind him, casually checking out his ass as he strides across the room.

Stopping at a high cocktail table, he looks back and motions for Darby to join him. After removing his suit jacket and draping it over a chair, he rolls up his sleeves and says, "Can you keep a secret?"

"Sometimes," she deadpans.

"I'm not really single."

Placing her drink next to his on the table, Darby asks, "Then why are you crashing a singles mixer?"

"Open bar." He smiles, as he runs a finger over Darby's wristband. "And why are you here, Holly Golightly?"

"Clearly I'm looking for a rich dude to take me to Tiffany's."

"Clearly." Slapping a small leather journal with an embossed peacock feather against the table, he asks, "What's your real name?"

"Darby," she replies, sipping whisky from her straw.

"Ah, much better." He opens his journal and scribbles the date at the top of the page. "Darby is a strong name for a protagonist."

"Why, thank you. Although I prefer the role of the reclusive villain." She leans forward and rests her arms on the table. "Are you writing a book?"

"In a way."

"So it's fiction?"

"Darby, everything's fiction once it's written." He cocks an eyebrow and nudges her arm. "But in this case, I'd like to believe I'm writing the absolute truth."

"Well aren't you a surreptitious flirt!"

Laughing, he replies, "I didn't mean to be vague!" He moves in closer and brushes his hand against her elbow. "Tonight is officially my last night of research – one year to the day since I started this project."

"I bet you use that line on all the girls," she teases.

"And it totally works." His playful smile fades as he adds, "But seriously, I belong to one woman, and hopefully," he holds up the journal, "this will win her back."

"Hmm." Darby pulls out her cell phone and opens her Gotham app. "I'm also here for some very important, life-altering research."

"Then let's toast to research," he jokes, clanking his gin glass against hers. "So what do you think about all this?"

"Meh, it's pretty lame. But it could be because of the time of year. January and February are like filler months." She stirs her drink and pokes the ice with the straw. "No one has a meet-cute in the winter."

"What's a meet-cute?"

"You know, a super cute story you can regale at dinner parties about meeting your significant other."

"And you think a singles mixer is the best setting for a winter meet-cute?"

"Oh, hell no. This is all staged." She sips the remaining whisky from her glass and adds, "I think winter is a time for pain and suffering. Hibernation. Regret."

"Ah, yes. The winter of our discontent."

Setting down her glass, she claps her hands together and applauds. "And the mysterious man quotes Steinbeck!"

He shrugs his shoulders as he writes something in his journal. "Shakespeare said it first."

Smiling devilishly, Darby suggests, "Do you think if we stand here together, drinking free booze and quoting literature, no one will approach us?"

Looking up from his notebook, he fights a smile. "Ah, like an experiment within an experiment. Let's give it a shot." He bumps her hip and quietly instructs, "Now laugh, like I said something hysterical."

Playing along, Darby places her hand on his arm and giggles. "How was that?" she whispers into his ear.

"A little forced, but it may buy us some time. Although, I'm not sure I can hold your admirer at bay for much longer." Cocking his head in the direction of a man walking toward them, he adds, "I'm Lucas, by the way."

"Nice to meet you, Lucas." Watching the suit approach their table out of the corner of her eye, Darby announces, "It's so nice to get out of the apartment without the kids!"

Following her lead, Lucas nods. "Tell me the name of your triplets again."

"Brenda, Donna, and Kelly."

The man in the expensive suit stops, grimaces in disgust, and then turns to walk in the opposite direction.

Darby clicks her tongue. "He must not like 90210."

"Yeah, but what if he was your perfect match . . . you just blew him off."

"He was nursing a Heineken. There's absolutely no way that guy could handle me." Darby chuckles while typing notes into her phone.

"Tell me honestly, do you think it's possible to find someone to love at one of these things?"

"Love?" She snorts. "Love is for the weak."

"How so?" asks Lucas, fascinated by her honesty.

"Have you ever been around two people in love?"

"Yeah, of course."

She slides her phone back in her purse and rolls her eyes. "Right, and they're all the same – fat and happy, but their souls are so fragile. People who live alone, eat alone, drink alone, have sex without attachment – the miserable and the hungry – they're the brave ones."

Lucas taps his pen against the table and chews on the inside of his cheek, but as he parts his mouth to argue against her provocative statement, Darby lowers her head and blushes.

"Didn't see that one coming, huh?" she mutters.

Taking a step closer, Lucas lifts her chin and stares into her watery eyes. "Your definition of love is a little harsh."

Darby snaps, "Well, what do I know?" She turns to face the bar and then leans back on her elbows. "I just know, that whenever I do *fall* in love, it will be with someone strong enough to pick me up and carry me away from loneliness."

"Is that what you really want?" Lucas probes. "Someone to rescue you from yourself?"

Allowing silence to answer his question, she finally says, "I need another drink. Do you want anything?"

Lucas shakes his head and replies, "I have a business dinner in twenty minutes, and I can't show up drunk again."

"Suit yourself."

She walks toward the bar and whistles for the bartender. Sitting on an acrylic chair that wobbles, she leans forward and gives her order. "Whisky neat."

As she waits for her drink, a man with graying temples and pale-blue eyes approaches the bar. She smiles as he takes a seat next to her.

"Hello, I'm Fitzwilliam Darcy. I think we'd make a great match, Holly."

"Oh, please. Do you actually use that cheesy shit?" She sneers, trying to rip off her wristband.

"Yeah, but it doesn't seem to be working at all tonight." He slides his finger under her band and asks, "Do you want help?"

"Nah, that's okay. I'll cut it off later." Grabbing her drink from the bartender, she throws it back and swallows. Slamming the empty glass on the bar, she wipes her mouth with the back of her hand. "What's your real name, Darcy?"

"Shawn," he answers quickly – either frightened or extremely turned on.

"Well, Shawn, order me another whisky neat while I grab my purse." She playfully walks her fingers up his forearm and then squeezes his bicep, gauging his sexual compatibility. "I'll be right back."

As she walks back to the cocktail table, Darby tugs at the corners of her glassy eyes. Realizing that Lucas is gone, she quickly scans the room, searching for the mysterious man who didn't even say good-bye, because to Darby, there's nothing worse than intellectual blue balls.

"Bass-stard," she snarls, picking up her clutch from the table.

But then she smiles, because stuck to the bottom of his empty glass, ripped from his journal of absolute truth, is a note.

Darby,

Love is strong.

LP

Chapter Three

Two hours later . . .

Outside the Downtown Marriott, Darby tightens the belt of her wool coat as Shawn hails a cab.

"Are you sure I can't give you a ride home?" he asks, sliding on leather gloves.

"No, really. I'm going to grab something to eat and then walk home." She points in the other direction with a wily smile, attempting to drop one last hint. "I literally live two blocks from here. Like, we could be there in five minutes."

But because Shawn is a gentleman, a Mr. Darcy who manages a hedge fund portfolio and plays racquetball in his spare time, he doesn't pick up on Darby's forward invitation to her apartment. He fits the criteria for a suitable shag – tall, rich, and emotionally detached – but sex with Shawn has the potential of being extremely boring . . . so, Darby says, "Anyway, I think I see a cab at the light."

Reaching in for a hug, Shawn pecks her cheek. "I had a great time tonight. You have my number, right?"

Darby pats her pocket and replies, "Got it stored in my phone." She nods toward the street. "Hey, a taxi pulled up."

"Let's try that new South African restaurant soon, Darby," he suggests, stepping into the street.

"Sounds perfect. I'll call you this week." She waves him off as he hops into the backseat of a yellow cab.

Continuing down West Street, famished and buzzed, Darby follows a couple playfully arguing over who will carry their grocery bags. She moves in closer, watching as they initiate a game of tug o' war with the handles of their bags. The man, wiry and tall, wins the battle, so he throws the canvas totes over his back in victory. Giggling, the woman wraps her arm inside his warm coat and nuzzles into his body. They stroll for two peaceful blocks, unaffected by the heavy snowfall, or the redheaded stranger trailing closely behind them. At the next block, they stop under a striped canopy of a luxury apartment building. Opening the door to their building, the man acknowledges Darby with a nod, and then dusts the snow off the sleeves of his wool coat.

Fucking snow, he thinks.

Darby returns his gesture with a shrug of her shoulders. *Eh, what're ya goin' do?*

(And that's how New Yorkers hold silent conversations with as little interaction as possible.)

After parting ways with the couple, she turns back and joins a group of anxious City employees combing the streets for the homeless. Furtively listening to their conversation, Darby pulls on her blue wristband until it breaks. She watches as the wristband falls to the ground, and then she buries it under the snow with the toe of her boot.

"Shelters are filled to capacity. We'll have to move displaced families to our contracted hotels," a young man reads aloud from his phone.

The group ducks behind a closed newsstand and studies a stack of file folders. Darby waits a few steps away, her head down, pretending to check messages on her phone.

"Hey, you," a woman shouts, walking toward Darby.

Snapping her head up in a panic, Darby replies, "Me?"

"Do you need shelter?"

Darby's cheeks redden in embarrassment as she shakes her head. She hurries to the crosswalk, just as the group of social workers hop into an unmarked, black SUV and speed away. Darby shrugs them off as well, because it's not her place to judge the eccentricities of the people or the city government.

Continuing across the street to her neighborhood drinking hole, she stops to peer through the foggy window. Inside the dimly-lit cigar bar, Darby spots her usual companions – Wall Street schmucks, politicians, real estate magnates, and the dozens of women who love them. Over the years, Darby has come to enjoy the efficiency of sex with a Downtowner – after all, time is money, and there's never enough of either one in New York.

She places her hand on the frozen door handle of the bar and gives it a pull, but then, a neon sign flickers and sizzles further down the block. Fascinated by its electric charm, Darby trots through the snow to check it out. As she reaches the vibrant window front of a casual restaurant, she reads the neon sign. "Meat Shop – No Vegans Allowed."

A woman clutching a takeout bag pushes open the door and asks, "Coming in?"

"I think so," Darby replies, catching the door with the heel of her boot.

Once inside the butcher shop turned restaurant, the heavy aroma of burgers and garlic fries tortures her empty stomach. Darby stomps her boots, forcing the snow to puddle on a mat, and then takes a seat at a butcher block table with two chairs. Smiling at the young family to her left, she removes her phone from her coat pocket to delete Shawn's number and return a text to Grant.

Darby: How quickly could you get a Gotham dating app on our platform?

Grant: It depends on the security perimeters.

Darby: Something really basic for the month of February – like a cupid tracker or some cheesy shit.

Grant: Rashid would need a few weeks. But honestly, there are so many dating apps with bad reps, why would we want to go there?

Darby: I think it's something to consider. Especially

But before Darby can finish her text, a voice with a thick New York accent asks, "Hey, gorgeous. Are you waiting for someone?"

Annoyed by the interruption and his pathetic pickup line, Darby lifts her head and heaves a sigh. But as her eyes meet his gaze, her scowl softens into a smile.

"I'm alone. Do you need the extra chair?"

Rendered speechless by her unspoiled beauty, he stares into Darby's sea-green eyes – hoping to catch a wave in the ocean of fortunate possibilities. "Wow, you're really pretty."

"Thank you," she says, admiring the way his flannel shirt fits snugly in all the right places. "Would you like to sit down?"

As his large hands clutch the frame of the chair, a group of men from a nearby table chant his name and tease him about getting laid. "I don't know them," he apologizes.

Glancing at the young family sharing an apple crisp, Darby whispers, "If you sit down, your friends will shut up."

"Doubtful." Sliding out the chair, he looks back at his friends and then sits down. "Are you really eating alone?"

"What do you mean?"

"Did I take your boyfriend's chair?"

"Uh, no."

"Husband?" Waggling his brows, he teases, "Girlfriend?"

"If you're asking if I'm single, yes, I am."

Drumming his hands against the table, he checks out her sheer sweater. "Great. Can I buy you dinner?"

"Surely my extra chair is worth more than the cost of a burger."

"I'll throw in an order of waffle fries," he deadpans. "What's your name?"

"Darby. You?"

"Anthony. Has anyone ever called you Shortcake?"

"No, never."

"I'm starving." Scanning the menu posted on a chalkboard hung to a brick wall, he smiles. "Should we order, Shortcake?"

Darby nods as a waiter wearing a rubber butcher's apron approaches their table. "Absolutely, Beefcake," she retorts.

"Kitchen's closing in an hour due to the storm. Do you know what you want?" The waiter pours two glasses of water and waits.

Craning her neck to read the board, Darby answers, "I'll have the Mexi-Cali burger with ranch dressing."

"And you?" asks the waiter, memorizing Darby's order.

"The Boom-boom 'shroom turkey burger, no mayo." Anthony takes a sip of water and then says, "And a large order of waffle fries."

"And two vanilla milkshakes," says Darby.

"Got it."

As the waiter heads back to the kitchen, Darby asks, "What do you do, Anthony?"

"I pick up garbage for the great city of New York." He leans back in his chair and chuckles, amused by her surprised reaction. "Impressed?"

"Maybe?"

Anthony's not really her type . . . but she just ordered a milkshake . . . so there's something about his beguiling personality and earnest banter that makes him appealing. It also helps that he's sexy as fuck.

"Department of Sanitation or a private company?" she asks.

"DSNY strongest." He flutters his dark lashes and props his chin on his hand. "Interested?"

Hell, yes, she thinks, shifting in her chair as not to seem too eager.

"Possibly." She smiles. "Can I ask some questions about your job?" Suddenly aware of the attention she's receiving from the nearby table, Darby sinks in her chair and lowers her voice. "Your buddies are watching us again."

"They've never seen someone as beautiful as you in real life." He glares at the table of his idiotic friends. Turning back to Darby, he runs his hand through his hair. "What would you like to know?"

"Oh, um, how do you handle the smell of rotting garbage in the summer?"

"Mind trick I learned on my Nonno's fishing boat," he answers without missing a beat. "And so you know, frozen garbage can smell just as bad."

Garbage man. Tall. Funny. Sexy. Single. Chin dimple.

Darby, mentally making a checklist, leans into him and smiles. "And what do the crazy people of New York like to toss away?"

Meeting her gaze, Anthony reaches across the table and tugs at the hem of her sleeve. "On a scale of coffee grinds to dead cat heads, how weird do you want my answer?"

Darby's eyes widen, revealing two blue sapphires gleaming with fresh luster. "Cat heads!"

With a small jerk of his wrist, Anthony returns his hand to his jaw and scratches his dark stubble. "Huh. Your eyes are blue. I could have sworn they were green . . ."

"They change color." She shrugs. "Tell me more about the garbage."

"I like them – your eyes."

"Thank you," she replies, sipping from her glass of water. "I like your, um, hair."

Anthony leans forward and tousles his umber-colored locks. "I condition daily." He smirks. "So, the trash stories?"

Darby sets down her water glass and nods. "Yes, please."

"Well, just this week, I picked up a family of mannequins, like the ones on display at Old Navy."

"That seems common, no?"

"Yeah, except they had gunshot holes. That's one freaky target practice, in my opinion." Anthony finishes his glass of water and slams it down on the table. "Sex toys are expected, but a few days ago, I found a box full of dildos with bite marks. Let me think . . . oh yeah, dentures inside a pickle jar, a Lilith Fair poster, a stack of pink Bibles, funeral flowers for Debbie, a canoe, oh, and four toilets."

"Wow, people have no shame."

"It's New York! No one gives a shit."

"Have you ever found anything valuable?" asks Darby.

"You'd have to define valuable."

"Ah, another man's treasure, right?"

"Right. I found a pretty sweet collection of Willie Nelson eight-tracks, and a buddy from my route found a Civil War musket. We're not allowed to keep anything, so we usually take the good stuff to Sully in the Bronx."

The waiter returns with their milkshakes and burgers. He places the baskets of food in front of each of them and then mutters, "I'll be back with the fries."

When the waiter returns to the kitchen, Darby says, "I wrote a blog article on the gentrification of urban garbage. It was actually very fascinating."

Anthony picks up his burger, allowing the mushrooms to ooze from the block of cheddar cheese. "Whoa, wait a minute." He takes a bite and chews slowly, toying with Darby's patience. He removes the straw from the milkshake and takes an icy gulp, and then sets his burger back in the basket. "You wrote about garbage?"

Slathering ranch on the top bun, Darby snorts. *I like him.* "Yeah, why?"

"Are you like a trash groupie?"

Darby cuts her burger in half, picks up a lone avocado slice and shoves it back inside. "Do you have groupies?"

"I have a few women who like to watch me toss their trash, if you know what I mean," he replies, waggling his brows.

"Not really."

Watching her take a large bite, Anthony says, "But I'm more than just eye-candy for the divorcees of the Lower West Side. I also restore mid-century modern furniture."

She places her burger back in the basket and wipes her mouth. "Now that's sexy," she purrs. "Scandinavian?"

His olive skin reddens as he sputters, "Oh, God, no. I'm a Robsjohn-Gibbings enthusiast. In fact, a few vintage furniture shops sell my walnut tables on consignment."

"I love window-shopping for furniture on Pinterest."

"Pinterest? You don't get out much, huh?"

Interrupting their conversation, the waiter delivers a basket of fries and the check. "Anything else before the kitchen closes?"

"Nah, I think we're good," Anthony replies.

As the waiter leaves, Anthony's friends approach the table. Leaning sloppily on Darby's chair, a short blond with a scruffy beard slurs, "Ant-man, we're headed out, bro." He takes the opportunity to stare at Darby's chest, sizing up her small, perky breasts. "Have a fucktastic night!"

Stumbling toward the exit, another friend knocks into Darby's chair and grabs a handful of fries. "Red, red, red," he chants, as he's pushed out the door.

"I met them tonight, I promise," Anthony apologizes.

She nods sarcastically. "They're just being protective of their pack."

"Yeah, they're decent guys." He shoves a handful of cold fries in his mouth. "So what do you do, Darby?"

Taking a quick drink from her glass of water, she replies, "I document humanity."

"Which means?"

"Um, I study cultures and societies within a city – specifically New York. I watch for trends and patterns of organization within the basic set of socio-factors; economics, family, politics, religion, gender, and now, the added influence of cyber socio-factors," she recites.

"So you're like a . . . ?" At a loss for the correct term, he waits for Darby to fill in the blank.

"Cultural anthropologist."

"Damn, sexy and smart! Do you write books?"

Darby lowers her voice. "I co-own Gotham Online – the one stop media platform for your Gotham needs. Human interest stories, apps, news, and a specified search engine."

"Ah, Gotham. I have the app." Snapping a finger and pointing in her direction, he adds, "You're Darby Wallace."

"C'est moi."

"You know a lot about New York." He wipes his mouth. "Where are you from?"

Confused, she replies, "Here?"

"Yeah, but where?"

"New York!"

"Seriously?"

"I grew up in Battery Park City with my dad and older brother. I lived in the Village for a few years after college, and now I'm back down here. What about you?"

"Well, I'm first-generation Italian, which means all my siblings and I were born in Queens."

"I'm picturing *Goodfellas*."

"Not exactly, but my parents do have a huge house in Whitestone with a marble door and garden statues."

Darby nods her head and asks, "Do you still live there?"

"Nah, it was a little cramped with my parents, my Nonno, my two older sisters, Sofia and Adrianna, my younger brother Vincenzo, and our three ugly cats. So now I share a two-bedroom in Bayside with my cousin Joey."

"Wow, that's a big family." She flips the ketchup bottle upside down and watches it drip. "I've never been to Queens."

"I'd be happy to give you the Q-tour," he offers. "How was your burger?"

"Pretty good." Darby places a napkin over her basket and asks, "Do you like your job?"

"I knew it!" He leans back in his chair and smiles. "You're a trash groupie."

"I've never met a garbage man!" Defending herself, she adds, "And part of my job is to ask a lot of questions – I guess I don't know when to shut it off."

"It's okay, Darby, I'd be impressed with me, too." Anthony chuckles and waggles his brows. "Yeah, I guess I like my job." And then his face softens. "But times are rough, and people are hurting."

"You probably see more than most New Yorkers can handle."

"Yeah, I've seen a shitload of forced evictions lately. I read in the Post that the landlords waited until the holidays were over. But now, families and veterans are getting kicked out of their homes while their furniture gets tossed on the street. They take as much as they can carry, but everything else is stacked and tagged for disposal."

"That's horrible. What do you do?"

"If I have my wallet on me and I see someone, then I'll give them whatever cash I have, but Darby, I'm required by law to remove any waste left on the curb."

"How are people expected to recover if they lose everything?"

"Oh God, the stories I could tell you would break your heart." He leans forward and plays with a straw wrapper. "A few months ago, we got a call from a sanitation officer to come remove trash obstructing a sidewalk outside a market. When we got there, an elderly store owner was in tears, lugging boxes of fruits and vegetables as quickly as he could back inside. Our orders were to dispose of everything on the sidewalk outside his store."

"All of the produce?"

"Yep." Anthony nods.

"Why couldn't you donate the food to City Harvest or something?"

Ashamed, he explains, "We weren't allowed. I can still see that old man's face, crying and begging us to leave just a few boxes of mandarin oranges for his grandkids."

"I can take a lot, but I hate seeing others in pain." Darby removes the cherry from her milkshake and pulls off the stem. "When it gets to be too much for me, I imagine alternate stories for strangers that cross my path. It helps muddy reality."

"I like to make up stories to explain why people do the things they do."

"Like crazy shit?"

Leaning back in his chair and crossing his arms, Anthony recalls, "There's a stop on my route I refer to as the Mad Artist."

"Ah, you give your strangers a name."

"Well, yeah, duh!" He smiles. "So every Tuesday, she throws out abstract paintings, not with a frame, just the fabric, you know?"

"The canvas?"

Anthony nods. "I think they're kinda cool, but the Mad Artist must hate them. They're always slashed and ripped, but stacked neatly in a pile and bound with a thin rope – like she feels remorse for her actions."

"So why does she do it?" Darby tips forward and rests her chin on her hand.

"Broken heart perhaps?" Speaking as if he's uncovered the truth, Anthony boldly claims, "Tortured artist with a fondness for white wine, and she has an uncontrollable internal rage. Definitely lives alone, doesn't know how to love, or maybe lost her only love. She drinks straight from the bottle while dancing to electronica music. And then once or twice a week, she purges her emotions – she breaks things, rips things, anything to recover her inspiration. And after finishing her last bottle of wine, she takes out the trash, and starts over. People need a clean slate."

"Wow. A clean slate," repeats Darby. "But how do you know Mad Artist is a woman?"

"I don't know, but I imagine Lauren Bacall with one of those long cigarettes, watching me from the window of her second-floor apartment."

"Lauren Bacall is no longer with us, rest in peace." Darby lowers her head.

Wiggling his fingers and dropping his voice to a ghostly howl, he jokes, "Which makes it even creepier." Anthony chugs back the last of his milkshake and then removes his wallet. "This place really emptied out, huh?"

"Yeah, and the waiters and busboys are staring at us."

"You ready to blow this joint?" Anthony places cash with the check and slides it under the ketchup bottle.

Getting up from the table, Darby puts on her coat and smiles. "Do you drink whisky?"

Anthony stands and reaches for his sweater and jacket from a nearby coatrack. "If it means I get to spend more time with you and possibly get you naked, then yes, I fucking love whisky."

"Good. I live across the street."

"Lead the way, Shortcake."

"I may look like a confident asshole who has his shit together, but I know, as soon as I hold my baby girl for the first time, she will own me."

Chapter Four

Grant Wallace is a self-made millionaire. After he graduated from Northwestern, he donated his winter coat and moved to the West Coast. With the advice and support from his father, Grant took an entry-level engineering job at a startup tech company in Silicon Valley. Of course, the company ran out of funding within eighteen months, but to his advantage, he had negotiated a contract that entitled him to a severance package if the company tanked. But instead of buying a condo in Palo Alto, or an impressive sports car, Grant used his cash payout to buy stock in several promising startups.

Shortly after his father's passing, when the market was right, and the timing was crucial, Grant packed up his surfboard and moved back to New York. The actual concept of Gotham Online evolved from a crazy idea he shared with his younger sister on the night of their father's funeral. But stuck in an unfulfilling job at the Museum of Natural History, Darby jumped at the chance to A) have an exciting career documenting the people of NYC, and B) have her brother back in the City. So in the summer of 2014, Gotham Online launched its platform with a collective group of young coders and engineers ready to revolutionize the way media is controlled.

And because he's responsible for almost everyone around him, Grant takes on the role of "all business, all the time." He wakes up every morning at five a.m., runs exactly two miles on the treadmill, empties the cat's litterbox, showers, starts the laundry, prepares a breakfast of gluten-free pancakes for his pregnant girlfriend, and then heads to the office located across the hall from his two-bedroom apartment.

On Monday mornings, Grant, the engineers, and the marketing team, conduct test runs on applications, and then strategize about new ways to expand their following. Around noon, Grant speaks to investors and potential buyers all over the world, ready to implement his platform in other metropolitan cities. Lunch is usually spent at Camille's doctor appointments, and then by three p.m., if it's a good day, Darby shows up like she runs the company.

The brother and sister duo are opposites in every way – often joking that they had different mothers. Grant is tall and charming, Darby is short and sarcastic. Grant's hair is smooth and black, Darby's hair is wild and fiery. But there's one thing they have in common – an insatiable thirst for fine whisky.

Running on time, Grant drizzles artisanal honey on a stack of pancakes, and then slices a banana to place on top. Arranging the plate and a glass of reduced-sugar orange juice on a tray, he carries Camille's breakfast to their bedroom.

"Babe, wake up," he whispers, as Camille slowly rolls to face him.

"I can't do this bedrest thing," she whines. Pushing herself up, she props her back against the headboard and shoves a pillow behind her neck. "I feel like a circus freak. We could sell tickets, Grant."

Smiling, he positions the tray over her lap and kisses her forehead. "Sell tickets to voyeurs wanting to watch a pregnant woman watch T.V. – Shia LaBeouf would be proud."

"I'm serious!"

Sitting next to Camille on the bed and gently placing his hand on her stomach, he smiles. "Five more weeks and we'll have our baby girl – you can do this, babe."

"Can I have ice cream for dinner? And none of that low-fat shit! I want Ben and Jerry's."

"I will get you whatever you want." Standing from the bed,

Grant grabs the remote from the nightstand and flips on the television. "Bathroom and kitchen only. Don't go to the deli, don't go to the post office, and please, don't go to Home-Goods to buy more things for the nursery."

"It's called nesting." Camille cuts the pancakes into small bites and sighs. "Don't forget to feed Bogart."

"Under control. I'll check on you later." He closes the bedroom door behind him and chants, "Here, kitty, kitty."

Bogart, husky and orange, appears in the kitchen doorway and circles Grant's leg. Purring loudly, he waddles back to his empty bowl near the refrigerator and waits. "You're not starving, buddy, that's for sure."

After feeding Bogart a can of grain-free trout medley, he pours coffee in his travel mug, grabs his instant oatmeal cup from the microwave, locks his apartment door, and then heads to Gotham's office.

Unlocking the door and spotting a shadow in the corner, he shouts, "Who's there?"

"Me, asshole." Darby steps out from the dark corner and flips on a desk lamp. "You're pretty wimpy, Grant. California made you soft."

"Hey, I was prepared to throw hot oatmeal in your face." He sets his breakfast on the conference table and crosses his arms. "Why are you here?"

Pulling her hair into a messy bun, she barks, "I work here, remember?"

"But why are you here *now*?"

"Jesus Christ!" she shrieks. "Does it matter?"

"All right, calm down." Grant takes a seat at the conference table and opens the lid to his oatmeal. "Shit, I forgot a spoon."

Moving to the small kitchenette, Darby opens every drawer until she finds a Taco Bell spork. "Here," she says, tossing it on the table. "How's Camille?"

"Sedentary."

Sitting across from her big brother, Darby opens a can of Red Bull and asks, "Any new names for the baby?" She guzzles the caffeine concoction without taking a break and then slams the empty can on the table.

"This week she's settled on Fern or Petunia."

"Awful." Darby scrunches her nose and shakes her head. "Destined to be a spinster who leaves all her money to feral cats."

"Don't say anything to Camille, please," he warns.

"I'm just sayin', you want me to be Aunt Darby, I'm going to need some cool names to work with. Like, Sassafrass or Elvira."

"I'll pass along the suggestions." Scraping the last spoonful of oatmeal from the cup, Grant adds, "Do you have something to publish today?"

"Dude, I was so lazy yesterday – complete wash."

"So you did nothing."

"Oh, I did stuff. Have you watched *Master of None* on Netflix? Three syllables, ad-dic-tive."

"I watched a few episodes." He takes a sip from the travel mug, and then leans back in his chair. "Camille's currently bingeing *Unbreakable Kimmy Schmidt*."

"I'm a lot like Kimmy," Darby deadpans. "Without Tituss."

"In no way are you like Kimmy, other than the red hair."

"Funny."

Tossing his garbage in the trashcan, Grant asks, "What about your dating app idea?"

Lowering her head with a tiny smile, she replies, "App or not, there's always someone to hook up with in Manhattan."

"Hookups are for the physically attractive and sexually deprived, Darby. Our followers want stories about real New Yorkers and legitimate ways to find someone to love. Didn't you go to that singles mixer?"

"Yeah, but I didn't stay long," she answers defensively. "And yesterday aside, I did manage to write something – quite charming, too."

"Can I read it?"

Darby stands from the table and retrieves her laptop from her desk. "It's a rough draft, and Sully's sending me some pictures, so it won't be ready until tomorrow."

"Who's Sully?"

"Georgie Sullivan, the king of Trash Castle." Darby sets her computer down in front of Grant and opens the document. "I met some sanitation guys the other night, and man, did they have some stories to tell," she says, carefully omitting the details about her night with Anthony.

Gotham Online

King of Trash Castle

By: Darby Wallace

Georgie Sullivan, a recently retired NYC sanitation worker, has been collecting unique items from his trash route for over thirty years. Starting with just a small locker full of collectables, Sully (as he's known to his friends) rented a warehouse floor in Harlem to display the NYC relics.

Organized by theme, a visitor can enjoy Christmas any time of year by strolling through the aisles of holiday decorations, or check out the thousands of nostalgic artifacts catalogued by type. And the museum has it all – pound your fingers on the dozens of vintage typewriters, bow to the shrines of Madonna (the singer not the Holy Mother) or Buddha, pose for photos with trophies, or take a child-like journey through the aisles of toys. At last count, Sully noted his collection of Furbies to reach the thousands. "I've considered placing batteries in all those creepy toys as a prank," said Sully. "But part of me thinks they could take over the museum if given the chance."

On a more sentimental note, the museum also displays salvaged photographs. "I look at the pictures a lot. Who are they? Where are they now? I kinda treat the people in the photographs as my friends," Sully admitted.

And who wouldn't? The Trash Castle of Harlem is more than just a museum, it represents a little piece of New York history. Open to the public by reservations only – and of course, monetary donations are encouraged.

Grant slides the laptop back to Darby and says, "Weird, but let's go with it. Can you get some pics inside this place?"

"Sully is sending me some promo photos he had taken a few months ago. Apparently, it's a hot spot on the Big Apple Tour."

"Ironic, no?"

"How so?"

"Tourists pay to see our garbage in a museum, yet complain about the smell of garbage in New York."

"There's the brother I love! I was concerned California changed you, but you're just as cynical as the rest of us."

"Don't tell Camille."

Darby nods. "If we're done here, I got people to watch and whisky to buy."

"Don't forget about the Miramax party tomorrow night. Which reminds me, you'll need the press pass."

"Oh, fucking A! I hate partying with the tarts from Page Six." Standing from the conference table, Darby closes her laptop and slides it into her bag. She takes another Red Bull from the micro fridge, and then grabs her navy anorak jacket from her desk. "Where's the stupid pass?" she huffs.

"Pinned to a schedule board in my kitchen," Grant replies, handing Darby a key to his apartment. "Try not to bother Camille, okay?"

Wrapping a plaid scarf around her neck she says, "Yeah, yeah."

She cocks her head to the side and smirks. "What would you do without me? I practically run this company."

Laughing, he professes, "*No one* thinks you run this company."

Mildly insulted, Darby shoots Grant the middle finger as she opens the door. He waves her off and then sends a text.

Grant: Darby's on her way over.

Camille: It's like 8:30. Did she sleep in the office again?

Grant: Probably. She needs an invite on the pin board.

Camille: Okay. I hear someone opening the door. And by the way, I want tacos for dinner. Like the Mahi-Mahi tacos from Rubio's in San Jose.

Grant: I'll see what I can do. STAY IN BED.

Ignoring his request, Camille Sanders carefully places the breakfast tray on the bedside table and shuts off the TV. Steadying herself with her elbows, she swings her legs over the edge of the bed and leans forward. She stands, keeping her balance by focusing on a wicker bassinet stashed by the window. Slipping her swollen feet into Grant's slippers, she takes a few cautious steps toward the bathroom to grab her robe.

As she scoots toward the kitchen, Camille watches as Darby rubs Bogart's belly. "You're the only person he lets do that."

"This cat is really fat, Camille."

"Orange cats are required to be fat and fluffy. Do you want tea," she asks, removing two mugs from a cabinet.

"Do you have that honey from the Seaport?"

"Of course," replies Camille, grabbing a jar of *Wild Honey* from the pantry.

Sitting at the large island, Darby lays her coat and bag on the stool next to her and loosens her scarf. "I'm sorry about dinner the other night. Grant had me go to a singles mixer at the Marriott."

The kettle whistles on the stovetop as Camille opens a wood case with an assortment of tea bags. "Green or black?"

"Green," Darby answers, unscrewing the lid to the honey and taking a whiff. "Maybe we can go out to dinner next weekend?"

"I wish, but Dr. Frink wants me on bedrest." Camille pours hot water into a pair of kitschy mugs, and then drops a tea bag in each. Handing off the Oakland A's cup to Darby, she asks, "So how was the mixer? Did you meet anyone?"

Drizzling a spoonful of honey into her tea, Darby laughs. "I met Patrick Batemen, Nick Carraway, and Mr. Darcy."

"What?"

"There was a literary theme," she explains. "I was tagged as Holly Golightly – can you believe that?"

"Well . . ." Camille shrugs. "I can see a little Golightly in you."

"No way!" Clicking her tongue, Darby glances at the time on her phone and says, "Shit, I need to get to Harlem."

"But you didn't finish your tea!" Pattering toward the pantry, Camille removes a to-go cup and its matching lid. Returning to the island, she transfers the tea into the cup while Darby puts on her coat. "At least take it with you."

"Okay, thanks." Ripping off the Miramax invitation from a linen pin board, she reads, "A movie about New York. Filmed in New York. And starring real New Yorkers." Scrunching her nose and tapping her chin, Darby asks, "Doesn't Tommy Barker live in L.A?"

"Yeah, Malibu. His bungalow was featured in People Magazine last month."

"Well, this should be fun," she grumbles, tucking the invitation into her bag. "Thanks for the tea, Camille."

"No problem. Stay warm!" she offers as Darby darts out of the apartment.

Finally, thinks Camille.

Because on most days, bedrest consists of eight hours entirely to herself. She can dance in the nude, eat broccoli and cheddar Hot Pockets, take long showers, binge-watch *Fixer Upper*, shop on eBay, and play jokes on Grant using a prank call app.

But today, Camille doesn't have time for Hot Pockets or naked yoga, because in four hours, she has a ticket to the matinee performance of *Hamilton* – and there's no way in hell she's missing it.

"I've seen the movie Taxi Driver a dozen times – it's like a rite of passage for a cabbie. New York during the seventies was a strange time. I mean, Travis Bickle had to clean cum and blood off the backseat of his cab . . . but the worst I've had to endure was melted froyo."

Chapter Five

By Tuesday morning, the weekend's powdery snowfall dissolves into a thick pancake batter of brown slush and street salt. So on a day like today, Groundhog Day to be exact, the people of New York must prepare for icy swamps, surprise potholes, wet feet, and a shitload of silly arguments over Staten Island Chuck's prediction. But for taxi driver Akash Rajeeb, life couldn't be better.

Heading south on Broadway, the twenty-something Bangladeshi raises the volume to a local rock station while finishing his buttered roll. He rocks out to the *Smiths* for a few blocks, and then lowers the volume when he spots a pair of businessmen signaling for a cab. Akash clears the meter and squeezes into a small space near a fire hydrant. As the two men file into the backseat of his cab, he looks over his shoulder and says, "Good morning."

Of course they don't respond – because to them, the aspiring street photographer with a degree in graphic design, who happens to drive a cab for extra cash, is simply a thread in the cultural tapestry of New York.

"Broadway and Wall," barks one of the men.

Akash rolls his eyes and taps the meter, never surprised by the blatant disregard of his existence. He listens to their harmless conversation about asset liquidation and mergers, and even chuckles when they make a raunchy joke. But as his cab waits at a light at the corner of Broadway and Wall, Akash almost loses his shit.

"Look at her, waving her arms like a mad woman," taunts the heckler from the backseat.

"Do you think she's mentally disabled?" the other asks, sliding his credit card through the reader.

Repulsed, he replies, "Definitely homeless."

"Something needs to be done about all the homeless people lowering our property value. Downtown is not like it used to be."

"We could round up all the trash and send them to Jersey," the other suggests with a devilish flicker in his eyes.

"I like her red hair, though. My second wife was a ginger, and holy shit, could she fuck!"

"Connie?"

"You know Connie?"

"She was my first wife – I introduced the two of you, Patterson!"

"Oh, shit, that's right." Opening the car door, Patterson warns, "Crap, she's coming toward us to panhandle."

Akash bites his tongue, and then, using an exaggerated Bangali accent, he says, "Thank you, kind gentleman sirs. Please take all your belongings as you exit the cab."

Grabbing the receipt, the two men hop out of the taxi, just as the crazy redhead climbs into the backseat.

"Hi," says Darby, placing a torn shopping bag from the liquor store on the seat next to her. "Did I just see Statler and Waldorf from the Muppets get out of this cab?"

Chuckling, Akash jokes, "I was thinking Randolph and Mortimer from *Trading Places*!"

"Oh, my God! Totally." Leaning forward to read the name on the license, Darby says, "Akash, I know this is a lot to ask, but my feet are wet, my bag is ripped, and I dropped my MetroCard over a steam grate. Can you drive me to Carlisle and West?"

Smiling at her through the rearview mirror, he raises the volume to the radio. "No problem. Is the music too loud?"

"Oh, God no, I love the Pixies." Darby exhales in relief and then hums along.

Pulling back onto the street, Akash starts the meter and says,

"Me too. They're performing in New York for the David Bowie concert."

"I hope it's televised – who can afford tickets anymore?"

"I know right? I like to photograph people going in and coming out of venues, that's about as close I as get to a show."

"Oh," Darby whispers, slightly alarmed.

Sensing her change in tone, Akash quickly adds, "No, no, no! I'm not a stalker! I'm a street photographer. My black and white photo series will be featured in an art show next month."

"Oh, well that's really cool! I'd love to check it out."

"March eleventh at the Spitz Gallery on Third," he boasts.

"I know it well – hey, just pull over here."

"You got that heavy bag, I'll take you to Carlisle," he offers.

"It's not that heavy, really, but my bag is splitting at the seam from the weight of the bottles."

"Why not use a delivery service?"

"Funny you should ask, Akash. I tried all my usual delivery places, but the earliest time slot available would be for tomorrow. And well, what if there is no tomorrow?"

"Because there wasn't one today. Bill Murray, *Groundhog Day*."

"Good one, Akash!"

Glancing at the meter, Darby slides her credit card through the reader and adds a sizable tip. "May I ask your age, Akash?"

"I'll be twenty-eight next month."

"Do you consider yourself a millennial?"

"Well, I enjoy social media and technology, but I wasn't born in this country. And I have no student debt, and I've never been to Williamsburg, Brooklyn. So what does that make me?"

"Refreshing," she answers. Sliding out of the cab and clutching her shopping bag, Darby leaps onto the sidewalk, barely missing a brown puddle of slush. "Good luck with your gallery exhibit!"

Beaming with pride, Akash waves, and then drives away.

Cradling her bag, Darby walks into her apartment building and quietly sneaks past the doorman. Even though she's thirty years old, and her father passed away two years ago, she often feels like she's being watched.

So why stay?

Her studio apartment is long and narrow, and her view is obstructed by scaffolding, but the original parquet floors and the impressive amenities make for a sufficient home address. And maybe it's because of the wonderful memories, or perhaps the prime location, but when the time came to sell the Wallace's three-bedroom condo on the sixteenth floor, Darby packed up her things and moved to the fifth floor.

Unlocking her apartment door and switching on the light, Darby unloads the four bottles of whisky and a bag of pistachios. She grabs a water bottle from the refrigerator, and then hangs up her coat and scarf on a rusty hook behind the door. Kicking off her damp shoes, and pulling off her wool socks, Darby takes out her phone to send Grant a text.

Darby: I have an idea for Gotham. What about a story featuring non-white millennials?

Grant: In a meeting.

Darby: And?

Grant: You're exhausting. Non-white millennials sounds harsh. Use "Millennials – the most racially diverse generation in American history." Schedule it for late February.

Finishing her water, Darby tosses the plastic bottle toward the garbage can. She watches as it hits a pizza box, teeters on the rim of the wire trashcan, and then rolls across the floor to the far corner. "Sonovabitch," she mutters.

Darby walks to her desk and powers on her laptop. Singing a *Pixies* song she can't get out of her head, she checks her emails, reads the comments for her most recent Gotham post, and then places a fifty-dollar bid on a Bahamas all-inclusive vacation. "Fingers crossed," she jokes, walking back to the kitchen to grab a glass and a bottle of whisky.

Glancing around her messy apartment, she briefly considers cleaning up before she has to get dressed for the Miramax party, but instead, she returns to her desk and pours herself a drink. Darby takes a sip, sitting in her chair and adjusting the headrest. Another sip to prime her palette, and then, taking a deep breath, she throws back the remaining whisky in a single gulp.

Pouring another shallow glassful, she types in a search for articles related to the DSNY. The first thing that pops up is the collection schedule during snow operations, so she scrolls past and clicks on a story from earlier in the month.

> *A twenty-six year old suicidal man leaps to his death, but was saved by uncollected garbage piles. The clinically depressed bus driver was worried he would soon be evicted from his apartment on West 46th Street where he lived alone. It's presumed he jumped from his 9th floor window early Wednesday morning with a note pinned to his chest. Although in critical condition, he's expected to make a recovery.*

Hand shaking, Darby grabs her glass and pulls it toward her chest. She clicks on a link to the NYC suicide prevention website, scrolling through the list of warning signs and possible triggers of depression. Pausing on the word, *loneliness,* she sets down her glass and wipes away the tears stinging her cheeks.

Jolted by fear, she scoots back her chair and stumbles toward the stack of paperbacks. Taking a deep breath, Darby falls to her knees and searches for the foil gum wrapper.

Dust bunnies, receipts, a broken piece of glass . . . an eyeshadow applicator, a ketchup packet, and a zebra-striped button. And then, shimmering between the pages of a worn copy of *The Sound and the Fury,* she finds the gum wrapper.

Chapter Six

Arriving two hours late to the Miramax party, plastered and unapologetic, Darby staggers into the lobby of the 48 Lounge. She rolls the unopened gum wrapper around the palm of her hand, smiling as a pointed edge jabs the inside crease between her fingers. Her odd behavior garners attention, so she's quickly whisked away by a security team. Frantically tucking the foil ball inside her purse and removing the invitation from her coat pocket, Darby announces, "I have a pass." She waves the card in front of the scariest security guard, fighting the urge to stick out her tongue.

Frowning, he takes her invitation and checks Gotham off the master list. He hands her a laminated badge and says, "Please wear your press badge once inside."

"Is there a coat check?" she asks, unbuttoning her long wool coat.

The security officer points in the direction of a tiny vestibule at the entrance to the lounge. "The film executives and the cast of *Prohibition* have asked that no photos be taken without approval."

"*Prohibition*? Fuck me!" she cackles.

He scowls. "No photos."

Saluting, Darby slurs, "Got it, officer."

Inside the vestibule, she removes her coat and drops it on the counter. Tapping a call bell repeatedly and clearing her throat, she yells, "Hello?" She waits, but no one appears. "I'd like a Big Mac with cheese. Hold the tartar sauce." Laughing at her own behavior, Darby tugs on the hem to her short, red silk cheongsam, and then clips the badge to the tassel of her purse. "Don't expect a tip!"

Ditching her coat, she makes her drunken entrance into the lounge. Staged as a Harlem jazz club with oddly placed furniture, she trips over a leather footstool and stumbles forward. A man in a 1920s tuxedo comes to her aid, holding her up as she swipes a fluted glass of champagne from an unattended tray. "Thank you," she says, guzzling the champagne.

Darby sets the empty glass on the nearest cocktail table, and then scans the room for an actual bar. She turns on the balls of her aching feet, cursing her three-inch Kate Spade glittery heels, and then proceeds to twist her skinny legs in an awkward ballet pose. Dragging her left foot in front of the right, she takes a cautious step toward a grand piano, balancing herself by pretending to wave to a female acquaintance. But to her surprise, an attractive man with a sarcastic smirk returns a single wave.

Darby clears her throat as she saunters toward him, taking in his broad shoulders and penetrating eyes. "Do I know you?" she quizzes, curling her ruby-stained mouth into a lazy smile.

"Yes, you do," he replies flatly.

Eyes glassy and lips pouty, Darby purrs, "I think I'd remember a night with you, big fella."

Laughing at her presumption, the man lifts his drink and taps his ring finger against the glass.

"Whoa," she takes a step back, "I'm not into married men."

"Okay?" he counters.

"Like ever." She crosses her arms and slouches, suddenly aware that she's a walking fireball with her red dress and ginger hair. "And even if you're a movie producer, I'm still not interested."

"Understood."

"So you're an actor?"

He shakes his head. "God, no. I'm a legal consultant."

"Well that's a major letdown," she huffs.

"What is?"

"You're a married lawyer."

Enjoying her refreshing candor, he asks, "Did you get what you need for Gotham?"

Curious yet cautious, Darby probes, "How did you know I work for Gotham?"

"Darby, right?" he confirms, removing his phone from his pocket and tapping the screen. Upon finding the proof he needs, a smile of victory creeps across his face. He shows her the screen, revealing a Gotham Online article from June 2015.

Darby squints her eyes as she reads aloud, "Brooklyn-based musician sets off for world tour."

"You had dinner at my house after an interview with my wife," he politely nudges.

Guessing at the memory, she recalls, "Ah, yes. Williamsburg."

"Cobble Hill," he corrects.

"Oh! Chloe! And . . ." Darby taps her chin and stares at his chest. "Ford!" she finally blurts.

Returning her enthusiasm with a thin smile, he adds, "Adam."

"Well, Adam, since we're old friends, how about you introduce me to the people I need to know."

"I can do that." Spotting Hollywood's rising golden boy, Adam places his hand on Darby's elbow and guides her toward the bar. "Whisky neat, right?"

"Yeah, but . . . Quick, tell me my favorite color!"

"Blue?"

Eyes wide as she carefully walks in a straight line, Darby squeals, "Holy shit! Are you sure you don't work for the NSA or something?"

"It was a guess, Darby."

Pausing by a group of vintage leather couches, Adam clears his throat and then flashes a friendly smile, because even though he's incredibly charming, Adam Ford is fiercely intimidating. "Tommy?" he says, approaching the starring actor of *Prohibition*.

Standing from his perch on the arm of the couch, Tommy Barker reaches in for a bro-hug. "Adam! Did you get the gift I sent?" he asks, his gaze focused on Darby.

"I did – although the wife won't let me smoke cigars in the house."

"Let her try one, she'll change her mind."

"I'll do that." Adam pats Tommy's back and says, "Hey, I'd like you to meet my friend Darby Wallace."

Tommy runs his eyes over the tight curves of Darby's dress and smiles, intrigued by her Chinatown bargain costume. "Hi," he says.

"Hi," she replies, her cheeks blushing.

"I don't remember seeing you on the set," he says. "What do you do, Darby?"

Enamored by Tommy's chiseled jaw, and thinking back to his last movie with a five-second shot of his bare ass, Darby mumbles, "Hum-a, Im-a, Gotham."

Coming to her rescue, Adam clarifies, "Darby owns Gotham Online."

"Oh, cool! I have the app on my phone," says Tommy.

"Really?" she asks, moving in closer to smell his cologne.

"Yeah – I used the restaurant recommendation tool last night," he says, taking a step closer to initiate a private conversation.

Observing their flirtatious body language, Adam takes his cue to leave. "Tommy, Darby, it was great seeing you both, but I need to get going."

Tommy briefly looks away from Darby and says, "Adam, man, so soon?"

"I have an early flight tomorrow." Gently grabbing Darby's elbow, Adam leans into her and cautions, "He doesn't drink."

Flinching slightly, she forces a smile as she hugs Adam. "Send my regards to Chloe."

"I will," he complies. "Tommy, it was an honor working with you on the film. I think it's your best work."

The two men shake hands as a server delivers Tommy a glass of tonic water with lemon.

"Can I get anyone else a drink?" he asks.

Fidgeting, Darby mumbles, "I, um, want, um . . ."

"Nope, I'm on my way out." Sending a text on his phone, Adam walks off with the server.

"Hey, I better see you at the New York premiere," Tommy shouts after him.

Adam looks back over his shoulder and nods, and then disappears into a crowd of people.

"How do you know Adam?" asks Tommy, leading Darby to an empty sofa.

"Oh, um, I wrote a Brooklyn series featuring his wife, Chloe. She's a folksy-rock singer – very cool couple."

"There's no way that guy is married to a rocker!"

Darby laughs as they sit down, her bare knee pressed against his muscular thigh. "Not only married, but they're totally into each other."

"Good for them," he praises. "So what else do you write about?"

Feeling slightly on edge and craving a drink, Darby fidgets in her seat while playing with her press badge. "Um, like New York anecdotes." She takes a deep breath, sighing in relief as a server approaches them with a tray of champagne.

"No, thanks, man. We're good," says Tommy, waving off the server as he places his tonic water on a nearby cocktail table. Tommy slides his arm behind Darby's back and sinks into the sofa. "I'm eight months sober."

"Because of your role in the movie?" She furrows her brows, trying to decide if his method-acting is worth her time.

"Huh? No, no. My character is a lawyer for an organized crime boss."

Hesitating, she asks, "Like AA or something?"

"Nah, I'm not doing the program."

"Oh. Rehab?"

Tommy runs his finger along Darby's upper arm and says, "I woke up one morning alone in a gas station bathroom and decided I needed a clean slate."

"Cold turkey, huh? That's um, very admirable." Biting her lip, Darby looks up into his dark-brown eyes and quietly admits, "I actually *do* drink. A lot."

"I figured. But here's the thing, Darby. I've been told I have an addictive personality." Tommy raises a hand and motions for a man in a suit standing by the bar. "Do you know what I mean?"

"Lemme guess, you're a workout junky," she flirts, running her hand along his muscular thigh.

Pulling her head to his mouth, he whispers, "I'm a sex addict."

Chapter Seven

Pinned beneath an assortment of down pillows, Darby shimmies her way from their suffocating grasp and falls to the floor. Thankful she's in a hotel suite with plush carpeting, she rubs her eyes and looks around the room. Still in her red silk dress from the night before, she makes it to her knees and then stands up, wobbly, but coherent.

Think, Darby, think. Unable to find her shoes or her purse, she patters around the large suite retracing her steps. Making her way to the bathroom, she looks for evidence of her actions from the night before. But instead, she finds a plush robe, a small basket of high-end toiletries, toothpaste, and a toothbrush. Wishing she had her big purse so she could nab the shampoo and facial cleanser, she washes her face and then brushes her teeth. Weary and confused, Darby twists her hair into a low bun and then carefully opens the bedroom door.

Interrupting a meeting, Darby lowers her head and tries to sneak past the conference table.

"Darby!" says Tommy, showered and dressed, and as handsome as ever. "Would you like some breakfast?" He stands from the conference table and guides her toward the small kitchen. "At least have some coffee."

Glancing at the spread of muffins and fruit on a table, her stomach growls. "Maybe just coffee and some fruit."

"Coming right up." He winks.

Watching as People Magazine's sexiest bachelor under thirty pours her a cup of coffee, she whispers, "This is weird."

"It's not weird."

"Maybe not for you," she teases, taking the cup of coffee. "What time is it? I can't find my purse or phone." Slapping her palm against her forehead, Darby moans. "And my coat. Shit! I left it at the party."

Taking a step closer, Tommy massages Darby's shoulders. "Relax. Nick has your things."

Slightly relieved, Darby swipes a mini blueberry muffin and asks, "So how does this work exactly? And who are those people over there?" She unwraps the muffin and lobs it in her mouth.

"Those people are my trusted circle of friends."

"But they're in your hotel room on a Wednesday morning."

Releasing a puff of laughter, Tommy explains, "We have to go over my calendar for the next few months."

"And what do the trusted friends know about me?"

"Only what they need to know." Tommy leans against the table and winks.

Darby returns a lazy wink as she finishes her coffee. "I should get going."

"Of course." Tommy kisses her cheek and then says, "Nick will drive you."

"I don't need a driver."

"Let him take you where you need to go. I insist." He takes the coffee cup from her hand and then leads her to the main door of the suite. "Would you like to visit L.A. next month?"

"Not really," she deadpans.

"Typical New Yorker." Laughing, Tommy opens the door and waves to Nick. In turn, Nick unlocks a door to an adjoining room and retrieves Darby's belongings.

Back in the hall, she steps into her glittery heels and winces in pain. Tommy helps her with her coat while Nick holds her tiny purse.

"Okay, I better get going," she says, belting her coat.

Reaching in for a long embrace and a kiss, Tommy holds her close and whispers in her ear. "Clean slate, Darby."

"Ms. Wallace, I have a car waiting to take you home. Please follow me."

She squeezes Tommy's hand and says, "Thank you." Taking a deep breath, she follows Nick to the elevator. After a jerky ride, they arrive in a secret underground parking garage where Darby is ushered into the backseat of a black Mercedes.

Nick sits behind the wheel and starts the car. "Tommy has requested I take you to the Gotham office." He passes back her purse and says, "I'm sure you will find everything exactly as you left it. I apologize for the measures we take to ensure Tom Barker's safety, but I'm sure you'll understand."

Snatching her purse from his hand, she rummages inside to check for her things. As they drive out of the garage, daylight streams through the sunroof with a powerful bolt. Darby pinches her temples and closes her eyes.

"Aspirin and a bottle of water." Nick passes a bottle of water and a package of aspirin back to Darby.

She reluctantly takes them and asks, "Why are you driving me to Gotham?"

"Well, I'm a driver obviously. And I like to monitor situations."

Swallowing back the aspirin, Darby pries, "And what's my situation exactly?"

"You spent the evening in the company of Tommy Barker, so now I'm taking you to your office in Tribeca."

"Forcing me to endure the walk of shame at the workplace, huh?"

"I monitor situations," Nick deadpans.

Glancing out the window at the piles of garbage yet to be picked up, Darby mutters, "You know, Nick, you don't have to worry about me. I'm writing a story on tax credits for filming production in NYC."

"I'm not worried about you – but you have friends."

She snorts. "I don't have friends." Removing her phone from her purse, she watches as the screen fades to black. "You can stop here."

Pulling over and unlocking the door, Nick turns around and

smiles. "I look forward to reading your post about tax credits, Ms. Wallace."

Darby opens the door and exits the car without responding or saying good-bye. Waiting for him to drive away, she flashes him the middle finger. "Monitor this, asshole."

Inside Grant's building, she waits for an empty elevator to enjoy in peace, and then takes it to the eighteenth floor. Avoiding the office and possible ridicule, she quietly knocks on the door to Grant's apartment.

Don't answer, she hopes.

A very bloated Camille opens the door. "Darby?"

"Hi, Camille. Can I come in and charge my phone?"

"Yeah, of course." Noticing Darby's bloodshot eyes and lazy posture, she adds, "Let me have your coat."

Shaking it off her shoulders, Darby passes the coat to Camille. "Where do you keep the phone chargers?"

"In the kitchen. Do you want coffee?"

"I'd rather have a whisky." Smoothing out her red dress and noticing a rip, Darby sits at the island and searches her purse. She eyes the little foil wrapper and moves it out of the way. "Where's Grant?"

Camille grabs a bottle of water from the refrigerator and passes it to Darby. "Across the hall I suppose. Are you okay, Darby?"

"Oh yeah, totally. I just need to charge my phone and then I'll go home."

"Stay as long as you need to." Busying herself with dirty dishes, she asks, "How was that party last night?"

"Oh, you know, just a work function." Darby plugs her phone into the charging station and waits for the battery light to flicker.

Unimpressed with her vague answer, Camille rolls her eyes. "Well, it must be fun to get dressed up and go to movie parties."

"Not really."

Camille and Darby don't have much in common, but they do have the potential of being great friends if they would allow themselves the freedom of perception. Darby lives her life with haste and embarrassing regrets – causing her to ultimately be defensive and weak. Camille, on the other hand, is a student of Buddhism – a philosopher of love and wisdom.

"So hey, I'd really like for you to come to dinner soon, Darby. I have a friend you should meet."

Powering on her phone, Darby asks, "Oh yeah? Who is this friend I should meet?"

"He's a doctor."

"Go on."

"Dr. Frink is tall and blond, and really funny."

Aware that Camille has very few friends apart from Grant's circle, Darby frowns. "How do you know Dr. Frink?"

Sitting down at the island across from Darby, she replies, "He's my OB."

"G-Y-N!" Darby sips her water and arches a brow. "That's a fetish disguised as a health occupation."

"He's a doctor."

"Who's a doctor?" Grant's voice booms with condescension as he enters the kitchen. Reaching for a mandarin orange from a fruit basket, he narrows his eyes and glares at his sister. "Surprised to see you."

Darby and Grant lock eyes, communicating via familial mind control. As Grant peels his orange and stares her down, she relinquishes her hold by blinking.

"Nice to see you too, big brother," she curtly responds.

"We were discussing Dr. Frink," Camille explains.

"Oh, sweetheart, I told you that idea would never work."

"And why not?" She sneers, itching to start something with her brother. "Maybe I'm interested in the kinky German doctor!"

"He's Bavarian," Camille quietly corrects.

Shoving the last slice of orange in his mouth, Grant takes a dig at his sister's character. "Because he's our obstetrician, a nice guy, and I'd like to keep him as a friend."

"What does that mean?" asks Darby, her cheeks reddening with each passing second.

"It means you'd rather sleep around than have a real relationship." Grant places his phone on the island and points to a photo taken at last night's party. "Tommy Barker? Really?" He grabs a napkin and wipes his sticky hands, and then tosses the orange peel in a tiny compost.

Flaming mad, Darby spews out her response like venom. "How dare you imply things you know nothing about, Grant! That's just a paparazzi pic taken outside the lounge, and if you were there like you were supposed to be, you'd be in the picture."

Feeling ashamed, Camille lets out a tiny whimper as she rubs her belly.

"Oh, there's more." Grant expands the screen to read the tag below the picture. "Tommy Barker has a thing for redheads. Caught in the City with a second piece of ginger arm candy just this week, the star of *Prohibition* is rumored to have a new addiction – gorgeous women. NYC Gossip columnist, Darby Wallace, was seen leaving his hotel suite this morning."

Not wanting to hear anymore, Darby interrupts, "So what? I'm an adult, Tommy's an adult . . ."

"He's a recovering alcoholic and a sex addict, Darby! And now Gotham Online is considered a gossip column, thanks to your crazy behavior."

"Grant, honey, lower your voice. There's no way Darby could have known she'd be photographed, and she would never try to hurt the image of Gotham."

"Stay out of it, Camille – I don't need you to defend me," snaps Darby.

"Don't speak to her that way! God, what has gotten into you?"

Rising from her seat and taking a step back from the duel, Camille grits her teeth. "You're both crazy."

Glaring at her brother, Darby seethes, "You know what? I'm really sick of your virtuous posturing – walking around like you save every goddamn thing in your wake. You have a hero complex, but heroes should be humble and strong. And a lot more attractive. With great one-liners and capes."

"For the record . . ."

"What record? Do you have a cape?" Darby snorts.

Leaning forward and pressing his white knuckles against the

cool concrete of the island, Grant clenches his jaw. "I did in fact save you. And I'm still trying to protect you from yourself."

"Yet where were you when Dad died?" she snaps, glancing in the direction of Camille.

Shaking his head, Grant fumes in anger. "That's not fair, Darby." He crosses his arms and takes one last dig. "It's easy to blame someone else when you're a selfish drunk."

Darby yanks her phone from the charger and stashes it inside her clutch. She reaches for her coat and tightens the belt around her waist. Brushing against Grant's shoulder with all the rage her tiny body can hold, she storms out of the apartment.

"Grant?" Camille whispers. "You basically slut-shamed your own sister."

"I'm so sorry you had to see that." He takes a deep breath and collapses against the island. "She makes me so angry."

"I know, but I'm really worried. She'll shut us off completely if we're not careful."

"What should we do? Have an intervention?" he says hypothetically.

Grimacing, Camille replies, "I think you just did."

"Shit, I had one shot with her and I fucked it up."

Several blocks away, Darby wipes the tears from her eyes as she enters an Irish pub. Upon seeing her friend and bartender, Paddy Hannigan, she forces a casual smile and takes a seat at the bar.

"You're early today," he quips, raising the volume to his radio behind the bar.

"You and your NPR, Paddy."

"It makes the day go by faster," he replies, drying off a set of mugs.

"Maybe. But I think you have a crush on Julia Pierce." Lowering her voice to a sexy purr, Darby imitates the introduction to NPR's most popular podcast. "Hello again, dear listeners. I'm Julia Pierce, your host of New York Love Stories. Join me as I explore our city of eight million people, one love story at a time."

Paddy pulls the lever to the tap and fills two mugs. Sliding one across to Darby, he says, "I'll drink to that."

"I don't want beer."

"Have a beer with me, Darby. I can't, in my right mind, serve you liquor before noon."

Frowning, she takes the beer and swallows back a frothy gulp. Slamming the mug back on the counter, she asks, "How does a bartender listen to the radio? Aren't you supposed to attend to the stories and problems of your paying customers – liquid therapy or some shit?"

"I got two ears."

A touristy couple enters the empty pub and sits at a table near the front window. Paddy whistles toward the kitchen, getting the attention of his niece playing on her phone. "Nan, bring them some menus."

She reluctantly stands from her perch and slides her phone in her apron. "Why would anyone want to eat here?" Nan remarks.

"Nan's a real gem, huh?" Darby teases.

"Ah, she's okay. One more semester and she'll be back in Boston." Paddy drinks his beer and then asks, "So what's on your mind?"

"I had a fight with my older brother. He's a certifiable asshole and completely wrong about me, but he's also kinda right."

"I didn't know you had a brother in the City."

"Yeah, Grant – tall, pale, and nerdy. He co-owns Gotham."

"Like Batman?"

"What?"

"Batman lives in Gotham."

"Holy shit!" She shakes her head in disgust. "Grant named the platform – he really does think he's a superhero."

"So what did Grant do to piss you off?"

"He called me a selfish drunk, among other things."

"Well, Darby, you are in a pub at eleven thirty." Paddy laughs, motioning to their surroundings.

"No offense, Paddy, but do you think I want to be in this shithole right now?"

"Of course not. This place is for tourists and salty old Irishmen who want to be alone."

"But I *am* alone," she whines.

"I've seen you with plenty of young lads."

"Right." She picks up her mug and mutters, "What do I owe you for this nasty beer?"

"How about this? You pay me the next time you're in here." He gives her a fatherly smile and a nod of encouragement. "Which I hope is never."

Standing from the bar and grabbing her clutch, Darby slides her mug back across the bar. "Your radio girlfriend fails to mention something very important during her weekly podcast. Most of us will never have a love story."

"Aw, now." Paddy slaps a dishtowel against the bar and smiles. "There's love to be found."

"Yeah, yeah."

As she leaves the corner pub, Darby pries open her clutch to search for her MetroCard. Finding the gum wrapper instead, she pinches it between two fingers and then tucks her purse under her arm.

She rolls the ball between her fingers as a food delivery bike speeds through the intersection. The wind shakes her balance, so she leans against a *No Parking* sign to regain her composure. Glancing at the pile of garbage at her side, and then down at the shiny wrapper, Darby makes a decision that will alter the course of her narrative.

Because in this moment, on that particular corner, only one block away from the fortress of strength, the grayness of winter shatters into tiny particles of something bigger. If only for a short time, the sun, taking its glorious cue, beams radiantly – shining down on Darby like a police interrogation spotlight.

"What's your next move?" it demands.

She stares into the blinding sunlight, inhaling enough warmth to thaw her wintery heart. Returning her attention to the wrapper, she carefully unfolds the delicate foil to the original rectangle. Taking a deep breath and closing her eyes, she chants, "Please be a number. Please be a number. Please be *your* number."

But before she opens her eyes to read Anthony's cell phone number, a group of tourists bump into her side as they rush to catch a tour bus. As Darby snaps her head in their direction, she loses her footing on the slushy pavement. Balancing her arms and leaning forward, a strong gust of wind sweeps in and robs her of her fleeting optimism. She stands motionless, watching as the paper floats in the sky, bobbing up and down like a cruel joke. Up, up and away – a silver speck of paper, a crucial piece of Darby's story arc ... gone.

"No!" she screams, seconds before she leaps in front of a taxi – seconds before the grayness of winter returns. And seconds before Akash Rajeeb will have the worst day of his life.

"I work in a trauma center, so I have enough crazy stories for a lifetime of dinner parties. But it's the faces of the family members I hold sacred – fear, worry, regret – no one wants to hear about the real stuff."

Chapter Eight

Dr. Joanna Nguyen clocks in her sixteenth hour in the trauma and emergency center at Mount Sinai Beth Israel. She chose this teaching hospital because of its neurology department, but sometime during her second year of residency, she found her calling as attending physician in the newly expansive ambulatory care.

Snacking on a protein bar in the tiny break room, she sends a text to her boyfriend, and then reads a published article from a friend about clinical depression to confirm her suspicion. She tosses her garbage in the wastebasket, slides her phone back in her lab coat, and then heads to room 107A to meet with the patient's family.

"Good morning, ladies," Dr. Nguyen greets the nurses station. "Is Patient Wallace ready to be discharged?"

They return polite nods and smiles while finishing the reports of the previous night's intake. Nurse Annie, young and pretty, replies, "I went over the discharge instructions with her and her husband. She's scheduled for a repeat MRI next week. Oh, and Patient Moskowitz pulled his catheter out again."

"Oh, geez. You know what, get a urology resident down here to fix it," Dr. Nguyen orders. Taking her computer tablet from the nurse's station, she opens the chart of Darby Wallace and quickly reviews all her notes. She writes a script for oxycodone, hesitates, but then saves it in the chart.

Approaching hospital room 107A, Dr. Nguyen knocks on the door and then pushes it open with her elbow. "Good morning." She extends her hand and adds, "I'm Dr. Nguyen, the attending physician for trauma and emergency care. You must be Mr. Wallace."

Grant stands from the plastic chair and shakes her hand. "I'm Darby's brother, Grant Wallace."

"Thank you for coming. Can we step outside a moment to discuss insurance coverage?"

Rubbing his eyes, Grant follows the doctor to the hall. She closes the door behind them and then leads him to an empty storage galley.

"I gave the nurse all of Darby's information. If there's a problem, I can pay," he offers.

"Oh, we have what we need on file. I actually wanted to ask you a few questions about Ms. Wallace, and maybe discuss her recovery plan."

"Okay," he says, crossing his arms.

"Are you the closest family member?"

He nods. "Our parents are deceased, so yeah."

"Boyfriend, girlfriend, roommate – anyone else spend significant time with Ms. Wallace?"

"She lives alone. I'm not sure she has many friends, or a boyfriend."

Dr. Nguyen scribbles a few notes on her tablet and then asks, "I know this is difficult to hear, but do you have any reason to believe your sister is suffering from depression or suicidal thoughts?"

Fear sets over his pale-blue eyes, remembering their last conversation and his nasty tone. "Our dad lost his battle with cancer two years ago next week. Darby was with him," he explains, trying to distract himself from crying. "I know the winter's rough on Darby, but suicide?"

"This next part is difficult." Lowering her voice to a gentle whisper, she says, "Witnesses claimed she jumped in front of the cab that struck her."

"That's not possible."

"She also had alcohol in her system, which I'm required to provide for the police report."

"She drinks, I'm aware of this." His posture changes and his mouth twitches.

"Again, I need to be thorough." Dr. Nguyen lowers her head to read the chart. "So about the drinking . . . with any head trauma, we like to run a full panel of bloodwork after the MRI scan. Ms. Wallace has a low platelet count, which is often times an indicator of liver damage." She writes the name of a doctor on her digital prescription pad. "I'd like to refer her to see a specialist, as well as a chemical dependency counselor."

Ashamed that he wasn't aware of the severity of her problems, Grant admits, "I came here expecting to find my sister with a laceration and a few bruises, but now you're suggesting medical treatment and therapy?"

"Yes." She nods firmly.

"This is crazy," he mutters, running his hand through his hair. "So I just take her home today and then hope for the best?"

"Ms. Wallace is being discharged, but she'll need to follow up with her primary doctor, and then a plastic surgeon regarding her sutures. And in a few weeks, another round of head scans will be ordered. Everything's detailed in the discharge instructions as well as a prescription of Percocet to help with the pain . . ."

"Is that wise? Giving her drugs?"

"Does she have a history with addiction, Mr. Wallace?"

Placing his hands behind his head and closing his eyes, he exhales through his mouth. "I don't know. God help me, I really don't know."

"Look, I get it. I have a younger sister whom I've had to look after our entire lives. She's frustrating and selfish, and I constantly have to lend her money." Dr. Nguyen pauses, choosing her words carefully. "Being the older sibling comes with a great responsibility."

Face ashen and body limp, Grant stares at his shoes. "I'm going to be a father very soon."

"Congratulations! Something tells me you'll make a great father." Dr. Nguyen tucks her tablet under her arm and places her hand on his shoulder. "Now, let's go chat with your sister."

Walking back to the hospital room, Grant manages to flash a comforting smile. This is his chance to make things right, and to show Darby she's not alone.

Scrolling through her missed texts and emails, Darby blurts, "This is my fourth day in this ugly dress." She stares at the rip on her thigh and cackles. "I bought in Chinatown because it was supposed to bring me good fortune."

Looking out the grimy backseat window of a cab, Grant asks, "Do you want to get breakfast? You must be starving."

"I really want to go home and take a shower. And brush my teeth."

Grant opens the discharge folder and reads from the list of instructions. "Washing your hair will be tricky."

"I know. Nurse Annie told me to wear a shower cap the first few days."

"Does your head hurt right now?" he asks, pausing on the disclaimer about pain medicine.

"Not really. My shoulder and back are killing me though."

"I can pick up some Advil when I get your antibiotic."

"Yeah, whatever."

Easing into the topic, Grant asks, "Did Dr. Nguyen go over your blood results?"

"She did."

"And you're going to follow up with your doctor?"

"I don't have a doctor."

"Darby, liver damage is some serious shit. You'll need to cut the alcohol, eat better, and monitor your platelet count."

"Thank you, WebMD. And for your information, liver damage

can occur from taking too much Tylenol," she snaps. "So stop giving me a headache!"

"I'm not picking a fight with you."

"Then like, shut up for a few minutes." She closes her eyes.

Riding in silence the remainder of the trip, Grant pays the driver and helps Darby out of the car. He carries the small plastic bag with the samples of bacitracin and hospital socks while following his sister. She seems so small and frail, and the dried blood clumped in her red hair freaks him out. He takes a giant step to meet her side and offers his arm. "Here, lean on me."

Without saying anything, Darby takes his arm and leans on him. The pair enter the apartment building and continue to the bank of elevators. Darby presses the button, whimpering as she extends her arm.

"The building looks exactly the same," he comments.

"You haven't been to my new apartment?"

The doors open and two men exit the elevator. Darby acknowledges them with a faint smile before stepping inside and pressing the floor number.

"I've never been invited," Grant teases.

"Well, here you go."

Reaching the fifth floor and unlocking the apartment door, the siblings step inside the boiling hot studio. As Darby flips on the switch and tosses her keys in a bowl by the door, Grant gasps in horror.

"Holy shit."

"Help me with my coat," she replies, shaking the heavy wool off her thin frame.

"Darby, what the fuck is this place?"

"Don't be a pretentious snot, Grant." She smiles for the first time in days. "Welcome to my humble abode."

Taking her coat and hanging it on a hook behind the door, Grant only breathes through his mouth. The dishes piled in the kitchen, the clothes thrown on the floor, the various mugs and whisky bottles reeking of fermented barley, and a garbage can overflowing with takeout boxes, are enough to make anyone dry heave.

"Where's your bed?" he probes, kicking a pizza box out of the way.

"It's a studio – I have a very nice sofa bed."

"And why is it so hot in here?"

"McToasty hates me."

"How much do you pay for this shithole?"

"Stop being a dick and pour me a drink," she barks, carefully sitting in the chair by the window.

Obeying her request, Grant steps over piles of laundry and heads to the kitchen. He rinses a glass and dries it with a takeout napkin. Returning with a glass of water, he asks, "Why do you have all those books?"

"They were Dad's. Is that tap water?"

"Drink it," he scorns, passing her the water. "I completely forgot about his collection of first-editions." Grant picks up a worn copy of *The Grapes of Wrath* and thumbs over the spine.

"Yeah. Aunt Ada was planning to toss them in the garbage."

"Well, I'm glad you kept them." He glances around the cluttered room, disgusted by the squalor, but impressed with Darby's commitment to melancholy. Standing over her desk, he opens her laptop and types in the six-digit password she's had since the tenth grade.

"Hand me that Jade Pearl menu on the desk," she says, closing her eyes and propping her feet on the coffee table. "And then be a good lad and pour me a real drink."

"I, uh, I can't do that, Darby." Being completely obtrusive, Grant clicks on her search history and scrolls through link after link of suicidal warning signs and clinical depression in winter. His voice shaky, he demands, "What is all this?"

Opening her eyes and sighing in exasperation, she says, "What are you grossed out about now?" Darby spots her opened laptop and glares at Grant, seething with fury. "Stop! You need to get the fuck out of here." She winces in pain. "Right now!"

Grant slams the computer closed and tucks it under his arm. "I'm not leaving without you," he says, his voice muffled by Darby's piercing shrieks and creative curse words. Ignoring her outburst, he opens the small closet by the bathroom and pulls out a fake Gucci duffel bag and a brown shopping bag. "You shouldn't be alone, Darby." Grant stuffs her laptop into the duffel bag and then rushes to her dresser.

"I swear to God, if you go near my dresser I will—"

"You'll what?" he chides, opening the top drawer and dumping the contents into the shopping bag. He proceeds to the next drawer as Darby launches an empty Gatorade bottle at his head. "Nice try, gimpy!" he teases.

"Oh, my God, I hate you so much!" Leaning forward and holding her breath, Darby carefully stands from the chair.

Hurrying to the bathroom, he clears out the cabinet above the sink. "Whatever else you need, we'll pick up at CVS."

Pissed and emotionally exhausted, Darby hobbles to the bathroom, begging like a child. "Please stop doing this. I don't want to go to rehab, or back to the hospital, or whatever your maniacal plan involves. Please, Grant. Please."

He sets the bags on the floor and pulls her into his arms, careful not to break her fragile shell. "C'mere, sis. It'll all be okay."

"I just want to be left alone," she blubbers against the sleeve of his coat. "I deserve to be alone."

"I grew up in an upper middle-class Italian-American neighborhood in Queens. Of course there were rumors of mafia ties, and yeah, my dad made a ton of money in the construction business, but I can honestly say, the only person guilty of some shady backhanded deal is my sweet, little mother. Her gnocchi has won first prize at the parish feast for over thirty years."

Chapter Nine

Pinching the edge of a ravioli square, Angelina Napolitano wipes her hands on her apron and then rolls out more dough. "There's some leftover *manigott'* in the fridge. But don't eat the chicken cutlets, they're for dinner tomorrow with Father Abruzzi."

"He's still alive?" Anthony takes a bunch of red grapes from the refrigerator as Angelina slaps the back of his head.

"Well, he's old, Ma!"

"Antonio, sit down and I'll make you a sandwich." She places her palm on his cheek and sighs. "You're too skinny."

"I'm going out later." He pops a few grapes in his mouth and then kisses his mother's cheek. "Can you fix the zipper to my jacket?"

Thrilled that her son still needs her, she replies, "Leave it on my dresser and I'll see what I can do."

"Thanks, Ma." He tosses the bare stems of the grapes in the garbage and walks to the living room.

Watching his grandfather doze on the sofa, Anthony flips off the television and then grabs his work jacket from the entry table. Carrying it up the stairs to his parents' bedroom, he tosses it on the dresser and quickly closes their door. Anthony has always been slightly freaked out by the statues of St. Peter scattered across the dresser, but it's the painting of St. Lucy and her plate of eyeballs that sends a chill down his back.

Running back down the stairs, Anthony meets his mother at the bottom of the staircase. She hands him an invitation and says, "Your cousin's wedding is April thirtieth."

"Lauren?" he asks, sliding the invitation in the pocket of his leather jacket.

"Marie. And she wants you to be an usher."

"All right, fine." He steps around Angelina and opens the front door. "I gotta go, Ma."

"Take the manigott' for you and Joey."

Nodding toward the street where he's parked his vintage motorcycle, Anthony shrugs his shoulders. "Can't do it."

"Oh, Jesus help me, I hate that thing."

Anthony hurries down the long sidewalk, closes the gate behind him, and then straddles his bike. Watching as his mother performs the signs of the cross, he fastens his helmet under his neck and laughs.

After a quick stop at his apartment to change his clothes, Anthony parks his bike on the sidewalk of Bell Boulevard. Every few weeks, he meets up with his buddies – a group of friends since St. Luke's grammar school. All of them are in relationships, and one friend has a wife and a newborn, so Marco rarely gets out anymore.

Anthony walks into the Beatles-themed bar and joins Lorenzo, Paulie, Angelo, Salvatore, and his cousin Joey. Pulling out a chair, he hangs his jacket over the back and sits down.

"What about you, Ant? Cancun trip in April?" Angelo pours Anthony a mug of beer from the pitcher and slides it across the table. "Paulie found an all-inclusive resort where the clothing is optional."

"Sounds good," he says, drinking his beer. "Are the girlfriends invited?"

Laughter erupts as Paulie punches Anthony's arm. "Why do you care?"

"Because it's weird being the only *chooch* without a girl, okay?" he growls.

"I thought you had a girl in the City," Joey teases.

"Eh, *ghiacchieron*," he grunts. "Who told you that?"

"Jimmy Polinsky told all the guys at work you left with a redhead last Saturday."

Anthony glares at Joey while the others wait for his answer. "You're all a bunch of rat bastards!" He laughs, trying to steer away from the topic.

"You got an Irish girl? Good for you," jokes Lorenzo. "But your ma's gonna be so pissed!"

"I heard she's one of them Downtown girls." Joey pours another glass of beer and adds, "Rich and snotty."

"Maybe she wanted to slum it with a garbage man," says Angelo.

"Nah!" The group of friends say in unison.

"*Disgraziat*," Anthony huffs. "I walked her home because it was late." He shrugs his shoulders. "End of story."

Oh, but it's not the end! What kind of love story would end when it's just beginning?

Chapter Ten

Under Grant and Camille's care, Darby spends the majority of her time sleeping. They wake her for a nutritious dinner prepared by a hired chef, which she refuses, and then again later for a Percocet, which she gladly accepts.

For two days, they drop everything to monitor her health and behavior – even taking turns to apply bacitracin to her cut. But on Friday morning, Grant must fly to Chicago for his standing appointment with an investor. Funding from major banks and companies gets him one step closer to filing with the SEC, and missing this meeting would be a major setback.

So early in the morning, he packs a small carryon bag, writes a note for Darby, kisses Camille on her belly, and then grabs a cab to Newark Airport.

A few hours later, awakened by the smell of bacon, Darby wipes the drool from her mouth. She tosses and turns in the guest bed, and then swats her face. Because not only did Grant leave her a note, he taped it to her forehead.

"What in the hell?" she mutters, ripping the single sheet of stationary from her head.

Sis,

Take care of Camille.

Darby wads the paper in a ball and tosses it in the garbage can. She rubs her eyes, stretches her arms, and then carefully crawls out of bed. Standing in front of a floor length mirror, she pulls back her hair to examine the laceration. Darby traces the jagged lightning bolt from her hairline to her ear. "Awesome." Then she pats the Florida-shaped bruise on her cheekbone and scowls. "Fucking taxi driver."

Completely famished, Darby shrugs her shoulders and apologizes to her stubborn reflection. "I'm hungry, okay? It's not like I'm giving in to their evil plans." So she grabs her sweatshirt and slides on her slippers, and as casually as possible, strolls to the kitchen.

Camille, dressed in yoga pants and a sweater, places a pan of crispy bacon on the stove top. Watching her pat the grease with a paper towel, Darby clears her throat to mask the sound of her growling stomach.

Turning to greet her, Camille says, "Good morning, Darby. Did you sleep well?"

"I had a dream about an orgy with the Night's Watch from *Game of Thrones*, so yeah, pretty great. Hey, can I get some aspirin or did Grant the narc hide that too?"

Moving to a cabinet, Camille takes two juice glasses from the shelf and says, "Funny, I thought you were here to police over me."

"How so?"

Camille pours orange juice in the glasses and then carries them to the island. "Grant hasn't left me alone longer than five hours in like six months." She opens a drawer and removes a bottle of Tylenol, tossing it to Darby.

With a tiny smile, Darby sits on a stool and pops open the lid to the aspirin. Shaking out three capsules, she swallows them back with the orange juice. "That bacon better not be vegan."

Laughing, Camille replies, "Can you keep a secret?"

And just like that, over crispy, peppered pork bacon, their friendship is formed.

Sitting on the sofa next to Darby with a bowl of Cheetos, Camille asks, "I canceled the chef for tonight, is that okay?"

"Oh, thank God! He used capers like they were tiny pods of caviar."

"I know, right!" Camille sucks the orange powder off her fingers. "How was your shower?"

"Refreshing. I love your shampoo." Darby sniffs a lock of her hair and sighs.

"It's the best. Grant doesn't understand why I pay so much for it, but yet his shaving cream costs twenty bucks." Putting down the bowl of Cheetos and grabbing a can of Pringles, she adds, "*Luther* or *Broadchurch*? They're both BBC detective shows, but one has Idris Elba, and the other has David Tennant."

"Idris Elba for sure," Darby replies, combing out her hair. "Have you watched everything on Netflix?"

Removing a stack of potato crisps, Camille shrugs her shoulders. "It's been a lonely pregnancy."

"I give you major props for the commitment."

"*Gilmore Girls* has eight seasons." Camille laughs. "If only I could've directed all those wasted hours toward something useful."

"Don't say that. You're doing something amazing," Darby assures, glancing at Camille's round belly.

Turning her head to look into Darby's eyes, she says, "Thank you for saying that."

"Can I ask you something?"

"Sure."

"I assume it's easy to hide the Pringles and candy bars from Grant, but how in the hell did you keep bacon in the refrigerator without him knowing?"

"I buried it under bags of kale." She picks up the remote and opens the Netflix app.

Sinking into the sofa, Darby recalls, "Did you know that Grant could devour an entire sausage pizza before he moved to California?"

"Really?"

"Oh, yeah, totally. When we were in high school, we'd order two pizzas every Sunday afternoon and then call my granny in Aberdeen. Dad and I would share a cheese pie, and Grant would eat one all by himself."

"I didn't know you grandmother still lived in Scotland."

"Well, she passed away five years ago."

"I guess Grant was a completely different person before he met me."

Sensing her change in tone, Darby replies, "Hey, I like post-Cali Grant a lot more than the prick he was as a teenager." Darby props a pillow behind her back and chuckles. "He was a delusional punk with a fake Scottish accent and Morrissey sideburns. I mean, the guy listened to Rancid and Green Day but sounded like Groundskeeper Willie – how punk could he have really been?"

Laughing hysterically, Camille rubs her belly. "He quotes *Trainspotting* when he's had too much to drink."

"Aye, you can take the Scot out of the highlands, but you can't take the Irvine Welsh away from their soul," she jokes, rolling all the necessary R's."

"Aye, indeed." Passing Darby a bag of Twizzlers, Camille eases into her question. "Are you doing okay? I mean, I know you're in pain from the accident, but how are you feeling?"

Darby removes a stick of licorice and nibbles on the end. "I'm wiped out." She brings her legs into her chest to rest her chin on her knees. "You know what's funny, I didn't even have my first taste of liquor until I was twenty three. Dad took me to a whisky bar to celebrate my new job at the museum, and then it sorta became our thing."

Lowering the volume to the television and turning toward Darby, Camille says, "Your dad was an amazing man. I only met Gordon the one time, but I know you're just like him. Stubborn, smart, and so funny."

"He was the best father," she says with a smile. "Grant may have been the prodigal son, but Dad and I were best buds."

"Losing him has been tough on you, huh?"

She chews on the inside of her cheek and closes her eyes, ready to confront her pain. "Stubborn is right. He wanted to die at home but he didn't want to be alone. So I sat in a chair by his bed and read to him for twelve straight days that February. We drank and laughed, and sometimes we even talked. But towards the end, he didn't know who I was . . ." Darby pauses, wiping the tears from her eyes. "And Grant wasn't going to make it in time to say good-bye, so I sat there and watched our dad take his last breath."

"Oh, Darby." She sighs. "Grant tried so hard to get to you, but the weather wasn't cooperating."

"Oh, I know. But I was never really mad at Grant." She lowers her voice to a whisper. "Maybe I've been jealous that he has you and I'm all alone."

"Well, you're not alone anymore. Even if all you get is a pregnant hippie and an overbearing brother, we love you."

"Oh, God. You heard me call you a pregnant hippie?"

"You also used the term Buddha Barbie a few times."

Rubbing her temple, Darby admits, "I've been such a bitch to you for no reason."

"Can I tell you something?"

"Sure, I guess."

"When we returned to California after Gordon's funeral, Grant outlined his plan to start a company in New York. I asked him if you'd be involved, and he said it was *your* idea." Camille pokes Darby's arm and smiles.

"Actually, my idea was to create a taco delivery app."

"I know! But I didn't flinch at the idea – I gave my boss notice, terminated the lease on my condo in Sausalito, and then bought a coat."

"You're too good a person to even be around someone like me."

"Hey, no more wallowing in self-pity." Camille takes a bite of a Twizzler as she rubs Bogart's belly. "I was stupid to think I could move here and we'd be automatic sisters."

Shrugging her shoulders, Darby says, "You know, we still can be."

Picking up her frosty glass of root beer, Camille lifts it above her head and clears her throat. "To new beginnings."

"Yeah, I dig that." Reaching for her root beer on the coffee table, Darby grimaces in pain. "Holy shit, my ribs hurt."

"Do you want a Percocet?"

"No, I'll need it to sleep tonight."

Camille sets her root beer back on the table and pushes herself up from the couch. "I'll be right back."

Assuming she's using the restroom again, Darby raises the volume to the television and restarts episode one of *Luther*.

When Camille returns, she sits on the arm of the sofa and places a hand on her side, gently massaging her pelvis. With a mischievous twinkle in her eyes, she says, "So, I probably shouldn't do this."

Arching a brow, Darby replies, "Should I be nervous?"

"No, of course not!" Camille whips out a plastic baggie with a joint and a lighter from behind her back. "Obviously, this stays between us. Deal?"

"Why do you have weed?"

"It's medical cannabis."

"What? No way."

Plopping down on the couch next to Darby, she explains. "When we visited my parents in the summer, I had the worst morning sickness. My dad took me to see his D.O. in San Francisco who then prescribed me medical marijuana."

"But you're pregnant!"

"Darby, it's not like I've toked up every night for the past five months. In fact, Grant smoked most of it."

"Grant Wallace?"

"Do you want it or not?" she asks, dangling the baggie in front of Darby's wild eyes.

Snatching the bag, Darby takes a whiff of the contents, and then crosses her legs. She pulls out the hand-rolled cigarette and lights the end. "Thank you."

"You're welcome." Camille pulls her leg under her body and shifts her weight. "Can I ask you a personal question?"

Releasing a long drag of smoke, Darby replies, "You can ask, but I may not answer truthfully."

"That's fair." She grabs her bowl of Cheetos and then turns toward Darby. "How was Tommy Barker?"

Coughing and laughing at the same time, Darby slaps her knee. "Camille, I didn't sleep with him!"

"But you made it seem like you did – and there were pictures."

"We were photographed, but trust me, we didn't have sex."

"Isn't he a sex addict?"

"Um," she takes a drag, "he's not a sex addict."

Scrunching her nose and cocking her head to the side, Camille says, "I'm confused. All the tabloids say he is."

"Tommy was an alcoholic, and during that time, the only acting jobs he could get were bit parts in movies." Darby rolls her neck and then continues. "So he sobered up on his own, but his clean image only made him less desirable by Hollywood standards. He's got that charming face and sweet personality, but he's also a trained actor – did you know he studied at Julliard?"

Camille shakes her head.

Focusing on the end of her blunt and blinking slowly, Darby says, "Tommy, the Hollywood bad boy became Tommy, the ABC Family star." She chuckles. "His fucking agent, greedy bastard in my opinion, started the rumor about the sex addiction."

"Wow, and he's okay with that?"

"His career's exploding!"

"Yeah, but at the expense of exploiting women for his own image. Don't you feel used?"

"Not really." She shrugs her shoulders.

Eyes wide, Camille slaps a pillow. "How can you not be pissed about this?"

Laughing, Darby answers, "Because I've been with guys who make Tommy Barker look like a feminist."

"Gah, I can't imagine what it's like to date in New York." She settles back into the couch and eats a handful of Cheetos.

"Honestly, I'm not sure anyone under forty actually dates."

"So people just hook up?"

"Well, yeah. Dating is for people who have ample time and resources." She takes another drag and smiles. "Think of it like this . . . I can get what I want whenever I want it, and that mindset applies to men as well. But there's also a race to find the good one before them other bitches."

"Grant's one of the good ones."

Faking disgust, Darby replies, "He is, I guess. How did you two meet anyway?"

"Oh, we met at kiteboarding lessons."

"Grant Wallace knows how to kiteboard?"

"Yeah! We were in the same group with hot surfer, Instructor Jeff." She tilts her head and chuckles. "Grant totally sucked in the beginning, and his pale skin really suffered in the sun for two days, but by the end of the weekend, I was so into him."

"Let me get this straight. You had a hot surfing instructor but you chose my geeky brother with the vampire skin."

"He was incredibly funny and humble, and he didn't try to show off like all the other guys I'd grown up with . . . in fact, I think he wore a life vest the entire weekend."

"And then you two started dating?" Darby holds in a puff of smoke and then slowly releases it.

"No, not then. We didn't even exchange numbers."

"Huh," mumbles Darby.

"I googled him – I mean, I remembered him mentioning Silicon Valley and Palo Alto, but he wasn't on social media or anything. I didn't know if he was even interested in me, but I had to find him, because he was the good one, Darby." Smiling, Camille rubs her belly. "And being Buddhist, I don't believe in fate. So after a month of checking every tech company's website, I finally called Instructor Jeff for Grant's info. And guess what?"

"What?"

"Grant was on the other line asking for *my* number!"

"Then it was fate."

Clicking her tongue and waving a cheesy finger, Camille replies, "Karma, Darby."

"Oh, right. And how is Karma different from fate?"

"Karma holds you accountable for your life. The ideology being, your current state is an after effect of your past actions. And your future state is an after effect of your current actions."

"Woah, that's really deep," she takes the last drag from the blunt, "or this is some strong shit." Darby places the joint on a plate and pulls her legs into her chest. "What if I told you I met the good one?"

"Are you serious?"

"Maybe. But I lost him." She rests her chin on her knees and pouts. "I guess Karma's not happy with my past actions."

Camille's blue eyes grow large and wild as her mouth curls into a smile. "We will find him!"

Around midnight, after finishing off a large, basil and pesto pie at the dining table, the two friends return to the living room to plan their search mission.

"Tell me everything you know about Anthony," demands Camille, as she eases down on the sofa.

Pushing up the sleeves to her sweatshirt, Darby stares into space with a goofy smile. "He's Italian. Dark hair and even darker eyes. This tall, maybe." She measures a height with her arm extended in the air. "What is that? Like six-two?"

"Do you know where he lives?"

"Um, Bayside or Whitestone, I can't remember. But he has a roommate – his cousin I think."

"And where does he work?"

"That I do know! He's a garbage man."

"Hunky." Camille giggles and then gnaws on a Twizzler.

"Oh, God, he oozes testosterone. But not in a piggish way. Anthony's kind and funny, and he enjoyed talking as much as fuck—" Darby clears her throat and lowers her head.

"Don't leave out the good stuff!"

Lifting her head and waggling her brows, Darby continues. "He's the best I've ever had."

"Then we call the Department of Sanitation and ask for a beefy Italian stallion from Queens named Anthony."

"Oh, yeah, I'm sure he's the only one." Falling back in an armchair and soothing her sore head, Darby exhales in defeat. "Just forget it, Camille."

"No way!" Camille reaches over her belly to grab Darby's hand. "Anything else you remember? Did he leave anything at your apartment that could be a clue?"

"Um, I caught a glimpse of the cell number on the paper before it blew away."

"Unless you're a math genius, that won't help us," Camille mutters, her speech slowing with each spoken word. "Close your eyes and try reliving the night."

Shutting her eyes, Darby replays their night together like a series of scenes from an off-Broadway play. Other than the canned laughter in the background as they deliver their jokes, every detail is exactly the same. But as Darby reaches the moment when she gives Anthony the gum wrapper, her recollection subconsciously alters the ending. She presses her fingers against his mouth, begging to be kissed. So Anthony kisses her, hard and deep, full of passion and yet so amazingly tender. He picks her up, a feather propped against his strong arms, and then carries her to bed. (A queen-sized bed, which she's never owned, but serves as a better setting than a Pottery Barn sofa bed in her tiny apartment.) And then they make love . . . gentle yet deliberate . . . and then rough and hedonistic . . . falling into each other's arms to watch the snow fall outside while discussing the proper way to apply a stain to walnut credenzas.

Opening her eyes and catching her breath, she shouts, "He restores mid-century furniture and sells it on consignment!"

Camille, sound asleep on the sofa, doesn't respond.

"Camille, you're sleeping," Darby whispers. Standing from the chair, she gently shakes her arm. "Let's get you to bed."

"Okay," she replies, rubbing her eyes. "Help me up."

Darby grabs her hands and heaves her from the sofa. "Come on, I'll tuck you in."

"Tuck me in," she snorts.

As the two reach the master bedroom, Camille removes her fuzzy sweater and climbs into bed wearing a sports bra and leggings.

Darby pulls the comforter over Camille and brushes a blond lock of hair from her face. Delicately kissing her forehead, she says, "Thank you for today."

"We'll find Anthony," she promises.

"I know." Darby smiles, realizing Camille is one of the good ones. "Good night, sis."

Backing out of the bedroom and closing the door, Darby quietly makes her way to the vintage liquor cart in the dining room. She crosses her arms and stares at the bottles of whisky and gin, her heart racing and her fingers twitching – but the suffocating grayness that haunts her winters has suddenly disappeared … because now, chapters into her story, Darby finally sees color.

Chapter Eleven

Awaking to the smell of bacon and maple syrup, Darby glances at the time on her phone and growls. "How in the hell does she do it?"

She rolls out of the guest bed, pulls on a sweatshirt, steps into her slippers, and then heads to the bathroom adjacent to the nursery. Staring at her cut in the mirror, she dabs a little cream on the itchy skin. She lifts her sweatshirt and examines the sizable bruise covering her side. "Damn. Where did that come from?"

After using the bathroom and washing her face, Darby heads to the kitchen and sits down at the island. "You're determined to make me gain five pounds."

"Good morning, Darby!" Camille chirps. "We have a busy day of sleuthing planned."

"Oh, yeah? I thought you were supposed to be on bedrest."

"Bacon?" she asks, arranging two slices of French toast on a plate next to an orange wedge.

"Always." Darby opens the bottle of aspirin and swallows back three capsules with her orange juice. "So how exactly are we going to find Anthony?"

"Um, well, you were right about the sanitation department being no help. They kept forwarding my phone calls to 311. A few people even laughed at me, but after a little research and mapping, I can determine that Anthony works out of the South Street Pier 36 depot."

"How long have you been up?" Darby pours syrup on her toast and arches a brow.

"Since five. But here's the thing, we can't just walk into the depot asking for Anthony."

"Then where are we going?" She takes a bite of bacon, watching as Camille floats around the kitchen like an elegant hippo.

"After you shower and dress, we're casing the consignment shops you mentioned last night."

"You actually heard me?"

"Uh, huh. I downloaded a list of the addresses of three shops that sell mid-century furniture pieces." She claps her hands. "Yay, I'm going to need a MetroCard."

"Do you think maybe the sodium and sugar overdose from yesterday is messing with your brain?" She takes a large bite of French toast. "Grant will freak out if I haul your ass around New York."

"Grant's stuck in Chicago until tomorrow." She removes a pan from a rack and asks, "Now, do you want egg whites?"

After a tortuous subway ride, the girls finally arrive in Gramercy Park at a vintage thrift store located in the basement of a church. Loosening the scarf around her neck, Darby helps Camille down the icy staircase to the store. Bells jangling, they push open the door and immediately file inside to escape the bitter cold.

"Time warp," whispers Camille, thumbing a velour pantsuit on a mannequin near the entrance.

With shoddy cell reception, Darby holds her phone above her head to check the store's website. "Clothing, furniture, décor, and housewares. We'll need to find the furniture section."

"Oh, my! You would look amazing in this black silk sheath, Darby." Camille holds the iconic cocktail dress over her body and sways side-to-side, humming the chorus to "Moon River."

"I told you, I'm not Holly Golightly." Darby takes the dress from Camille and returns it to the rack. "Let's go to the back."

Making their way through the racks and shelves of clothing, the two women stop at a display case of vintage jewelry. But it's not the baubles and sparkle that catches their eyes, it's the wall shelf lined with at least a dozen, colorful reminders of their youth.

"Caboodles!" they screech in unison.

Darby points to a mint-green one and says, "I had that exact one – until Grant used it as a tackle box for a fishing trip with his Cub Scout troop."

"Oh, wow. I hope the other scouts made fun of him," Camille deadpans. "I had that hot pink and black one – très L.A. chic." Distracted by something, she hurries off toward a case of Styrofoam heads. "Darby!"

Following the shrill of her voice, Darby joins Camille in what is clearly the wig section. "Ew, are these used?"

"Hello, do you need help with a wig fitting?" asks a man, late-forties and sporting a handlebar mustache.

"Oh, no, we're just browsing," replies Camille.

"Have you considered the fun you could have as a brunette?" he charms, staring at Camille's Rapunzel-like braid.

"I have considered brown hair, like an alter ego!"

"Yes, exactly," he says, waggling a brow.

"I'm sorry, but are these wigs used? Because that seems, well, super gross." Darby examines a blond shag while Camille asks to see a black angled bob.

"To answer your question, wigs can be resold. It's become a lucrative business for Orthodox Jewish women to trade and sell expensive wigs."

"Interesting. And what are the prices of your wigs?" Darby probes.

"Well, most of these are new and a very high quality, so they're a bit pricy for consignment."

"I really want a wig," Camille mutters.

Patronizing her friend, Darby says, "Hey, you buy whichever one you want while I check out the furniture."

As Darby makes her way to the back, her phone buzzes with a text.

Grant: Make sure Camille takes it easy.

Darby: She's watching TV.

Grant: Okay. Good. I'll be back tomorrow afternoon.

Darby: Buy me a tin of Garrett popcorn.

Grant: Okay.

Darby: So hey, hypothetically, can I take Camille to dinner tonight? Somewhere close.

Grant: Not a good idea. Just order takeout.

Feeling guilty, she tucks her phone in her pocket and pretends she didn't ask. Finding the section of vintage furniture, Darby sits down in a chartreuse armchair and glances at the price tag. "Three thousand dollars?" she exclaims.

"Can I help you with the Dunbar chair?" a man asks.

Startled, Darby swallows air. "Oh, um, is this chair mid-century modern?"

A smile forms beneath an equally fascinating mustache as the man in the wig department, but then quickly disappears when he notices the sutured gash on Darby's head. "It is. An Edward Wormley addition to Dunbar furniture during the fifties. It's in excellent condition with a chic velvet upholstery. Chartreuse is very on trend."

"I totally dig it," she says, standing from the chair. "What about tables?"

"Occasional tables? Are you looking for mid-century?"

"Yes!" Her eyes grow wild as the man strokes the tip of his mustache.

"We don't have any mid-century tables on consignment this

week, but I do have a few rattan and cane side tables I picked up from an estate sale." He points to two tables in the corner collecting dust.

"Oh, God, no. I'm searching for something specific, like Rob and John Gibbons."

Furrowing his bushy eyebrows, he corrects, "Robsjohn-Gibbings?"

"That's them!" replies Darby, snapping her finger.

"Well, we rarely get any of his pieces on consignment. You might try Furnish Green on Broadway," he mumbles, moving on to another customer checking out a pair of lamps.

Turning on her heels and removing her phone to search for Furnish Green, she whispers, "You've been most helpful, Burt Reynolds." As Darby makes her way to the front of the store, panic sets in. Camille is nowhere to be found . . . not with the wigs, not in the dressing room, and not waiting by the door by the armless mannequins. Darby scans the store, wondering if in fact this shop is legitimately non-profit. *Mental note: research non-profit consignment stores. And twins with matching mustaches living in Gramercy Park.*

"Darby!" Camille shrieks.

Following the sound of her high-pitched voice, Darby spots a beaming Camille disguised in a short black wig. "I didn't think you were serious," she says, as she joins her friend.

"Oh, I never joke about wigs." Camille shakes her head, allowing the fringed bangs to dance above her sparkling blue eyes. "I feel sexy and mysterious. You should get one!"

"Maybe next time."

"Did you find any of Anthony's furniture?"

"No, but I have the address to another store on Broadway."

"Broadway," repeats Camille, petting her shiny synthetic locks. "Furnish Green?"

"Yep, that's it. Are you ready to go?"

"Yes, but first, I got you something." Camille pulls out a small velvet bag from her purse and passes it to Darby. "They made me think of you."

"I can't even imagine what, in a thrift shop, would make you think of me," she teases.

"Actually, these are for your alter ego, Holly Golightly." Camille giggles, opening the door to the street and embracing the freak encounter of February sunshine.

Sliding out a pair of slinky, elbow-length silk gloves, she arches a brow. "I'll wear them to my next dinner party." As they walk toward the train, Darby tucks them in her pocket.

"Wear them now, silly!" urges Camille.

"You're insane!"

Complying with the wiles of her pregnant friend, Darby removes her fingerless gloves and slides on the vintage silk accessories. As the two women descend the steps to the subway, they hold their heads up high and smile – Camille slithering down the steps like a Broadway siren making her musical debut, and Darby, well, she's unknowingly starring in her very own New York love story.

Flipping the price tag to a walnut hutch and gasping at the number of zeros, Darby whispers, "Camille, I don't think we'll find anything in here."

"Who would pay eight hundred dollars for an ashtray?" Camille picks up an orange clam-shaped bowl and shakes her head.

"Can I help you find something?" a young woman dressed in a sequin vest and gaucho pants asks.

"Oh, hi." Darby shoves her gloved hands in her pockets and forces a smile. "Do you have any consignment furniture?"

The woman laughs. "Oh, you're serious?"

Annoyed by the sequined snob, Camille curtly replies, "Specifically walnut coffee tables."

"Everything in our store is handpicked from auctions and estate sales. We also serve as a showroom for high-end designers."

The woman motions around the small office tucked inside the Empire State Building. "We rarely have more than twenty pieces in the showroom, but I could put you on a list for coffee tables."

"No, that's okay. I'm searching for a certain style that's been refinished."

"If you want consignment pieces, then you need to go to Williamsburg," she scolds.

"Right," Darby answers, scowling as the snot walks away.

"Did Anthony mention any shops in Brooklyn?" asks Camille.

Running her silk fingers through her wild hair, Darby sighs. "I don't know. This entire week is a blur." She delicately strokes the gash on her head as she stares at a velvet armchair similar to the one she owns.

Camille yawns and rubs her side. "Let's map out the subway route to Williamsburg."

"Oh, Camille, you look exhausted. You should go back to the apartment and rest."

"But I want to help you find Anthony." She yawns again.

"I'll meet you back at the apartment in a few hours. Don't worry about me, okay?" Darby takes Camille's hand and squeezes it gently as they take the elevator down to the lobby.

Walking toward the street, Camille rips off her wig and shoves it into her bag. After a slew of occupied cabs, a taxi finally slows to a stop. Turning back to Darby with a tiny smile, she says, "Maybe it's time to use your secret weapon."

"Which is?"

Camille slides into the backseat of the cab and rubs her belly. "Make Anthony come to you."

"It's not that easy, Camille."

"Yes, it is." She smiles and then glances at her watch. "You've got two hours alone, Darby, and then I'm calling police."

Darby shuts the door to the cab and watches as it drives over a Wendy's bag full of ketchup. Looking away, she pulls out her phone to search for consignment shops in Brooklyn. As she expands the map of their location, she's swept into a group of tourists lining up for a double-decker Big Apple tour bus.

"What the hell, people?" she shouts as she tries to break free. But when an older gentleman loses his balance on the curb, he pulls her with him toward the steps of the bus.

"Hopping on?" the tour guide asks, finishing a bottle of coconut water.

"What? No!"

"Plenty of seats up top!" he jokes, failing to ask her for a ticket.

Huffing in frustration, Darby slides into an available seat with plans to hop off at the next stop.

As the bus fills to capacity, the tour guide switches on his headset and says, "Okay, Driver Mike, we're all set." He taps the shoulder of a lady lingering by the staircase. "Ma'am, I'm going to need you to take a seat."

Following his orders, she plops down next to Darby and pulls out her tour map. "Did you go to the top?" she asks.

"Pardon?"

"The Empire State Building! It always makes me think of *Sleepless in Seattle* – so romantic."

"I've never seen it," she lies.

The speaker above Darby's head crackles and hums as the tour guide starts his rehearsed speech. "Thanks for hopping back on Big Apple Tours. I'm Will, born and raised in the Bronx, and our driver is Mike G. from Jersey."

Several tourists in the front few rows applaud after Will's vibrant introduction.

"Stop number ten is Madison Park. Coming up on our left is the iconic Flatiron building constructed from steel in the beginning of the twentieth century. And because of its unique design, the building frequently hosts art exhibits in the prow."

Heads turn to the left to snap photos of the building converging at the triangular intersection, including Darby's seatmate.

"Oh, wow!" she exclaims, reaching over Darby to take a picture.

Continuing with the history lesson, Will reveals, "The original elevators were hydraulic and slow as shit, and ladies, the building didn't have women's restrooms during the early years . . . but that's what you get when it only took four months to construct." Will taps on Driver Mike's shoulder as he pulls into the stop. "Anyone hopping off at twenty-three skidoo?"

Darby, unsure if she should raise her hand or whistle, misses her opportunity to escape.

"Are you visiting?" the woman next to her asks.

"Huh? Oh, no, I live here."

"Oh, my God, you're so lucky! I love New York. This is my fifth visit as an adult – my sister came with me this trip."

"It's a great place to live."

"I bet it's just like *Sex in the City*, huh?"

Not wanting to ruin her optimistic view of what it's really like to live in Manhattan, Darby nods her head.

"We're from a small town in Wisconsin – everything closes at ten p.m. I'm Carol, by the way."

"I'm Samantha," lies Darby, turning to look out the window.

As the bus jerks and swerves to the right, Will grabs onto the stair railing. "Easy there, Driver Mike." He reattaches his headset and continues the tour. "Our next stop is in the heart of the Village, otherwise known as the bohemian capital of the East Coast. Like everything else in New Amsterdam, the Dutch gave this village its own name. Groenwijck, which means green district, eventually evolved into Greenwich."

"Did you ever watch *Felicity*? Most of the show was filmed around here." Carol snaps a few shots of a row of brownstone-ish apartment buildings.

"Greenwich is also home to New York's first penitentiary. Soon after though, the inmates were sent up the river to Sing Sing," remarks Will.

"Huh, that's interesting." Carol chuckles. "Up the river, I get it now."

"Do we have anyone wanting to hop off and enjoy an early dinner or a trip to the Whitney Museum?" asks Will, looking around the bus full of tourists.

Carol raises her hand. "Me, me, me!" She stands from the seat bench as the bus slows to a stop. "Bye, Samantha!"

"Bye," says Darby, missing her chance once again at a getaway.

"Okay, Mike, let's step on it," jokes Will. "Stop twelve is one of my favorite places in the summer. Washington Square Park is an open space for New Yorkers to relax and play a game of chess, but the history behind this potter's field is quite grim."

Spotting a Big Apple street sign, Darby stands from her seat and shouts, "I want to hop off here, please."

"Mike, we got a hopper." Will smirks as he steps to the side, allowing Darby to squeeze past him.

Returning a polite smile, she says, "Thank you. It was most informative."

"Watch out for crack dealers and hookers," teases Will.

Darby rolls her eyes as she jumps from the bottom step to the sidewalk. Bypassing the crowds congregating at the fountain, she heads to a pretzel cart packing up for the evening.

"Hey! Can I get a pretzel with mustard?" Darby asks.

"Lady, as you can see, I'm done." The vendor shuts off his propane tank and unlocks the wheels to his cart.

"Just one pretzel – I'm so hungry." She flutters her lashes and smiles, working her charm to no avail.

Shooing her away, he barks, "Try Greene Street. Frankie leaves at seven."

"Awesome," she replies, darting off toward Greene Street.

Arriving at the hot dog cart, Darby catches her breath and orders, "One pretzel with mustard, please."

"Five dollars," says Frankie, lifting the pretzel off the heated carousel.

Darby hands him cash in exchange for a warm pretzel, and then pockets a stack of napkins. "Thanks," she says, ripping open the mustard packet with her teeth.

Joining the stream of Downtown commuters, Darby unintentionally follows an attractive couple on a romantic stroll. While walking at a leisurely pace, she carefully squeezes a fine line of yellow mustard along the crusty edge of her pretzel – a trick every New Yorker masters by the time they're a teenager. As she takes a bite, she eavesdrops on the couple's conversation about a recent engagement. (The woman hopes for a July wedding, but the man suggests autumn.)

Darby rips off a small section of the pretzel with her teeth, but the couple stops abruptly, causing her to drop the opened mustard packet and extra napkins on the sidewalk. "Sonovabitch," she mutters.

Stepping over her trash and moving to the side, Darby watches as the romantic spectacle unfolds. The woman squeals, bringing her hand to her mouth and dramatically feigning a crying attack. Intrigued by her sudden excitement, Darby follows the woman's gaze toward a storefront with large glass doors flanked by decorative white columns. And not just any storefront, she's standing in front of the most iconic jewelry store in New York City.

Impressive, Darby thinks.

The man, smiling proudly, kisses the woman on the cheek as she wipes her eyes. "Let's find your ring," he says, leading her toward a shallow staircase. On cue, the doors open. And they glide into the jewelry store like passengers on a cloud to the magical land of diamonds and platinum.

Shrugging her shoulders, Darby steps under a blue canopy protecting a display window of sparkling gemstones. Never a fan of expensive jewelry or the little blue box, she instead stares at her reflection in the window.

The winter sun has set, but as a streetlight illuminates the window, she can make out her wild hair, swollen eyes, and chapped lips. And as her eyes fall on the reflection of her silk gloves holding a salty pretzel, she laughs – a deep, belly chortle with no regrets.

Because just like Holly Golightly, she belongs to no one, a slob with no name . . . and yet, she realizes she wants it all.

Darby takes another bite of the pretzel, trying to remember the appropriate quote . . .

"Everything's better at Tiffany's," she mutters as she chews. "Nothing bad could ever happen at Tiffany's?"

But because this is New York, land of the competing follies, tourists crash her *Pretzel at Tiffany's* moment to take selfies with the gemstones.

Hashtag little blue box, Darby thinks as she walks away from the SoHo store.

With her head held high, she heads north toward the nearest subway stop. A gust of chilly wind swoops in and propels her forward, urging her to hurry. So at the next block, she catches up to a sanitation truck clearing out the heaps of snow garbage. Darby stops to watch, amazed by their efficiency and strength. And within minutes, New York's Strongest offers the people of New Amsterdam a clean slate.

Buzzing with a renewed energy, Darby tosses her trash in a garbage bin and then sends a text to Camille.

Darby: I'll be there in 20 min.

Camille: Good. I ordered dumplings.

Darby: Do you have keys to Gotham?

Camille: Yes! Why?!!

Darby: You were right.

Chapter Twelve

Gotham Online

Pretzel at Tiffany's

By: Darby Wallace

Today's post contains a trio of open letters addressed to 1. Singles (women, not the movie) 2. Taxi drivers 3. DSNY.

I know what you're thinking, "When did Gotham become so smug it posts critical editorials?" Well, it's not Gotham Online, it's me, Darby Wallace. And after the indescribable week I've had (i.e. meeting and losing the good one, getting hit by a cab, and reliving a scene from Breakfast at Tiffany's) it's safe to say I deserve a pass.

To the single women of Gotham:

Did you know that some women outside of New York envy our lifestyle? As if we shop and brunch and drink cosmos! Well, you can thank the gals from *Sex in the City* for that misrepresentation.

I know, I know . . . it can feel invigorating to experience independence as an adult in this town. We relish alone time, but we can just as easily fill the void by traveling or focusing on our careers. And it's a great time to be single and sexually progressive – no more slut-shaming or frowns of disapproval from the old harpy down the hall. You can thank the gals from *Broad City* for that one!

But I wonder, as many of you do as well, do we enjoy our freedom so much so, that we fight the urge to fall in love? Can we, in theory, have both?

So here's my challenge . . . buy a pretzel or a bagel, or even a cup of bone broth, and then head straight to Tiffany & Co. There's magic in that storefront window, you just have to look.

To the cab drivers of Gotham:

The douchebags that litter the backseat of your cab and yap on their phones don't see you, but I do. I see the photos of your kids taped to the dashboard. I see your weary eyes after an eleven-hour shift. I see your smile when the tip is bigger than 2%. And I see you struggle to provide for your families.

Please, at the next intersection, turn to the dickwad in the backseat and repeat after me – I AM A PERSON.

To the Department of Sanitation:

Thank you for clearing the snow garbage from my street. Also, I'm in search of an Italian beefcake who's not embarrassed to sing the lyrics to "Boys Don't Cry."

MUST BE: Employed by the DSNY. 25-35 years old. Single.

MUST HAVE: Hair the color of Nutella. Eyes the color of a Starbucks java frappuccino with a caramel swirl. Fuzzy, shag carpeting covering his chest. A dimple on his chin. And a perky butt that looks good in poly/cotton work pants.

REQUIRED SKILLS: Speaks fluent Queens-Italian. Knowledgeable in the history of cereal boxes. Good with his hands. Polite when it matters. And indecent when it matters most.

So if you know of a man who fits this description, go to him and say, "Anthony, ya boombot, go to her."

"So? What do you think?" asks Darby.

Turning on her side and kicking the duvet off her legs, Camille scrolls through the post for another read. "I think it's raw and beautiful with a touch of your unmatchable humor. And I don't know how you do it, but you speak for a generation of women who are often misjudged." Her eyes grow large and animated as she adds, "Just look at all the comments!"

Darby glances at the laptop and laughs. "I've had ten marriage proposals and a dozen men offering to be Anthony the garbage man."

"Creeper alert! You should ask Rashid to create an extra secure firewall or something."

"Who's Rashid?"

"Rashid! He maintains the security for Gotham?"

"Oh. I'll stop by over there on my way out for coffee. Do you want anything?" Darby closes her laptop and slides it into a bag.

"I'm doing a rapid cleanse today before Grant gets home." Camille tosses in the bed, trying to get comfortable, and then wedges a pillow between her legs. "I'll shower and then clean up the apartment."

"I cleaned the apartment last night – all signs of junk food, bacon, and marijuana have been removed."

"You're the best! Then maybe I'll sleep just a little longer," drones Camille, closing her eyes.

Backing out of the bedroom and shutting off the light, Darby whispers, "Sweet dreams."

She stops in the kitchen to feed Bogart, wipes down the counters for a third time, and then starts the dishwasher. Lazy as ever, the chubby cat circles her legs and purrs before plunging his head into the ceramic bowl.

"Thanks a lot," Darby snarls, gathering the wad of orange fur plastered to her jeans. She grabs her coat from the hall closet and folds it over her arm, and then locks the apartment door behind her.

In the hall, she bumps into an engineer from Gotham. "Hi, JP," she says, opening the door to the office.

"Hey." He removes his skullcap and shoves it in his coat pocket. "What did you post at eight a.m.?"

"Um, like an open letter, I guess."

Worried that he missed a meeting, he asks, "Was it scheduled?"

"Well, no." She drops her coat on the receptionist's desk and crosses her arms. "Is there a problem? I assumed that a post on a Sunday morning wouldn't interfere with the other stuff."

JP laughs as he removes two Red Bull cans from the fridge. "The other stuff?"

"Look, I just write silly shit about New York. All that algorithm and back pinging stuff is like a foreign language to me."

"Pingback," he corrects.

"See? That's an odd word."

They sit down at a long table covered with laptops and buckets of Twizzlers while JP removes a hard drive from his bag. "Your post has been up for three hours and has over two hundred thousand hits."

"Wow, that's great, right?"

"It would be great if we were prepared."

"Oh, I'm really sorry, JP. Does Grant know?"

"I did get a text from him about twenty minutes ago."

"Should I retract the post?"

"Darby, that post is everything!"

"I'm so confused." She props her head up with her arm and collapses on the table.

"Chuck and Amanda are coming in to help me set up search perimeters. If we can keep people on the site after they read your post, and incorporate the needs of our investors, then this could work for us." Glancing at his phone, JP adds, "Holy shit, five hundred thousand hits and counting."

"Crap, now I'm feeling emotionally exposed."

Ignoring her complaint, he instructs, "You'll need to do a follow-up post tonight."

Standing from the table, Darby grabs her bag and watches as JP furiously types lines of code. "Follow up with what exactly?"

Shifting his attention to his phone to read a text, he waves her off. "Just post anything. It doesn't matter."

Trust me, it matters, she thinks.

Carrying a cup of coffee, and a gluten-free bagel for Camille, Darby reaches in her coat pocket to remove her buzzing phone.

Grant: I'm proud of you, sis.

She doesn't respond, but instead, saves the text to her cloud as a reminder of his compliment.

Hopping into the elevator with a young family, she smiles at the toddler sucking on the end of a blanket. "My, what a beautiful pair of shoes you have!"

The little girl's eyes light up as she clicks the heels of her ruby slippers. "Tank you," she mutters.

As the doors open, Darby and the parents nod politely. She exits the elevator and walks toward the apartment. Fishing the keys from her pocket, she unlocks the door and calls out, "Camille? Grant?" Setting the coffee and bagel on the kitchen island, she leans down to pet Bogart's head. He purrs and falls on his back, begging to be scratched on the tummy. But his purrs begin to sound like moans, deep and shallow with a burst of desperation.

Panicked, Darby rushes to the bedroom and kicks open the door. "Camille?"

"Darby?" Her response is weak as she uses all her strength to squeeze a pillow between her thighs. "Something's not right."

"Oh, my God! Should I call 911?" Darby fiddles for her phone, but her fingers go numb and useless. Afraid to get too close, she falls to her knees next to the bed and reaches for Camille's hand. "What can I do?"

"Grant will be here soon." Camille grimaces in pain. "And Dr. Frink is on his way over."

Surprised that doctors make house calls, Darby asks, "Should I keep the front door propped open?"

"Bogart will run out." Camille clutches Darby's hand as tears roll down her bloated cheeks. "I think I hear Grant."

Unsure what to do, Darby dabs Camille's face with the sleeve of her sweater. "Stay calm, and like, breathe."

Luckily, Grant bolts through the door and runs to Camille's side. "Babe, Dr. Frink seems to think it's sciatica." He sits on the side of the bed and strokes her back. "Is it painful here?" he asks, kneading his knuckles into her hip.

"Yes. Is Dr. Frink coming soon?"

Grant glances at Darby kneeling on the carpet and says, "Can you wait by the door and let him in?"

"Yes, of course," Darby replies, standing from the floor and rushing out of the bedroom.

Feeling ashamed about her latest adventures, Camille takes responsibility by revealing her secrets, "I saw *Hamilton* last week.

And Grant, I bought a short black wig." She squeezes her eyes shut while rolling on her back.

Confused, Grant positions a pillow under the small of her back and says, "Okay."

"What I mean is, I bought a black wig in Gramercy Park. Yesterday. After I ate bacon."

But before Grant can ask a dozen questions about her shopping trip to Gramercy Park, Dr. Frink quietly knocks on the door to the bedroom. "Hello, Camille," he greets, placing an iPad and a blood pressure cuff on a dresser. "The first thing you need to do is roll on your side to alleviate the pressure on your back."

"But my hips hurt," she cries.

"Let's try your side again." Dr. Frink moves to the bed, observing as Camille arches her back, scoots down the mattress, and then flops her top-heavy body to the right side. "Good. The second thing you need to know is, this pain you're experiencing is all very normal and will not harm the baby."

As Camille relaxes, Dr. Frink presses different spots on her stomach to feel for the placement of the baby. "Everything looks good, Camille. You can apply a warm compress for today."

Lurking in the doorway, Darby whispers, "I'll just wait in the living room." She closes the door just as Dr. Frink mentions a pregnancy girdle.

Grabbing her cup of cold coffee from the kitchen island, Darby stomps her foot. "Bogart, get off of there." She pushes the cat off the armrest of the sofa and then she takes a seat in the center. Bogart curls up in a ball and lies at her feet, purring against the toe of her boots. Removing her phone from her pocket, she scrolls through the hundreds of comments following her Gotham Online post. No sign of the real Anthony, but several remarks give her pause.

> Thank you Miss Darby for liking the taxi drivers. We are people too. Many blessings.
>
> I'm a 34 year old single woman living in Brooklyn and I

completely agree with your thoughts about wanting it all. Why is it so difficult for men to get that?

You suck Darby Wallace! You're a lesbian with tiny titties!

S/W/M/31 Italian beefcake living in College Point.

I have all the answers! Join me in this exciting new study!!! Earn $$$ and vacation $$$ from your home. SKDFJOJdjfaldsfjwj skdjfasdjwb n dfkjaskdlf http://flowerfood.com

Startled from his slumber, Bogart hisses as Grant and Dr. Frink walk through the apartment.

"Call the office tomorrow and Sherry can help you schedule an appointment with a chiropractor. Other than the things we discussed, we have to just let this ride out."

"Keeping her off her feet is the problem," Grant huffs.

Darby twists her torso and rests her chin on the back of the sofa, practically invisible to the men in front of her.

"Bring Camille in on Thursday," requests Dr. Frink.

"Will do. And thank you for coming over on a Sunday. A phone call would have been enough." Grant shakes his hand as they walk toward the door.

"Just don't tell any of the other patients, okay?" he jokes. "See you Thursday."

As soon as he leaves, Grant heads straight to the liquor cart in the dining room.

Annoyed that she's being ignored, Darby clears her throat. "Well?"

Pouring himself a glass of scotch, Grant glances at Darby and laughs. "Oh, Darby, you're still here?"

"Um, yeah."

"Do you want a drink?"

Darby turns back around and crosses her arms. "I haven't had a drink in five days."

"Wow! You're taking that liver scare seriously, huh?" Grant sits down in an armchair and crosses his leg.

"I'm taking myself seriously for a change."

Acknowledging her strength, he says, "Good for you."

"What's going on with Camille?"

"Her poor posture and the baby are putting pressure on her nerves."

"That sounds painful."

"It is. And she'll need to stay off her feet as much as possible for the next few weeks." He narrows his eyes. "Which means no schlepping around New York for wigs and furniture. But I'm glad you two had so much fun the past few days."

"You're lucky to have her, Grant."

"And she's lucky to have you, Darby." He swallows back the rest of his scotch and then closes his eyes. "God, I'm tired. But I should probably go across the hall and check on Gotham."

"Nah, you should spend the day with Camille. I can check in and then pick up groceries for dinner."

Opening his eyes and shaking his head, he asks, "What happened to the chef?"

"Oh, um, he got a better job."

Grant scratches his head and then shrugs his shoulders. "He did seem a bit flaky."

"Yeah, it was the best for everyone, really."

"Oh, before I forget," he says, tossing her a set of keys.

She catches the keys midair and shrieks, "You had my keys with you the whole time!"

"Purely by accident – I promise. But you should go home . . . you're ready."

"You mean, you're ready for me to leave."

Grant leans forward and rests his elbows on his knees. "Darby, listen to me, you're always welcome here."

"Yeah, yeah." Standing from the couch and stepping over Bogart, she pats Grant's shoulder. "How about dinner this week?"

"Yeah, yeah. You always say that."
"But this time, I actually mean it."

Arriving at her apartment building around five p.m., Darby stops by the leasing office to inquire about a two-bedroom rental. She takes a free booklet as Margaret, the leasing manager for the building, shuts off her computer and frowns.

"Can I help you?" she grunts.

"Oh, I live in 5G."

"Yes?" Margaret stands from her desk and grabs her coat from the rack. "I'm on my way out – do you have a maintenance issue?"

"No, no." Darby opens the booklet and asks, "Are there any two-bedrooms available?"

"We may have a few opening up in the spring – but you're in a studio now, right?"

"Yeah, I have a studio. But I was thinking of maybe buying a larger unit and getting a roommate."

Margaret passes Darby a business card and smiles. "Buying in this market is definitely a wise move." She shuts off the lights to the office and directs Darby toward the door. "Stop by tomorrow around noon and I'll show you a gorgeous corner unit on the tenth floor."

"Okay, great! Thanks." Darby slides the card into her coat pocket and then heads to the bank of elevators.

Outside her apartment, she drops the Gucci duffel bag on the floor and jams the key in the doorknob. Carefully opening the door, Darby flips on the lights and mumbles to herself. "Just because you live alone doesn't mean you have to live like a pig."

Kicking shoes and dirty laundry out of the way, she puts her laptop on the desk and then opens the blinds to her window. She knows what she has to do, so she hurries to the kitchen to find a box of trash bags and a tub of Lysol wipes.

She sets her supplies on the table and then hangs her coat on the door hook. Pulling her hair into a ponytail, Darby rummages in the hall closet for empty boxes. She finds three, all from her last move, and carries them to the kitchen. One by one, she rinses the empty whisky bottles and places them in a box, all twenty-six of them.

Darby returns to the closet to get two laundry baskets. She picks up the piles of clothes and sorts them by color, realizing that her dark colors basket is twice as full. "I need new clothes," she huffs, scooting the baskets against the wall.

Planning to recycle, she hauls the boxes of empty liquor bottles outside her apartment and lines them up by her door. "Now the garbage," she declares, returning to the kitchen. Wrestling with the roll of black trash bags, Darby eventually rips one from the pack and shakes it out. The method of disposal is as follows:

Trashcans – empty

Refrigerator – clear out and prep for healthy food

Desk – organize and declutter

After tying off three large trash bags, Darby hauls them to her door and stacks them in a pyramid. Wiping her brow, she pulls off her sweater and tosses it in the laundry basket. Sitting down at her antique desk in her bra and jeans, she opens her laptop to check the delivery options for Bed, Bath & Beyond. She fills her shopping cart with new sheets and pillows for her sofa bed, a floor lamp, picture frames, a broom, a vacuum, dish towels, and a Nespresso machine with a starter pack of espresso pods. Tapping her chin while gazing out her window, she remembers that Crate & Barrel will deliver furniture in Manhattan for a decent price.

She scrolls through the website in search of a real bed, but her mind is set on a gorgeous bookcase with glass doors similar to the one her grandmother had in Scotland. Cringing at the price tag, Darby takes her emergency credit card out of her wallet and completes the purchase.

As if he somehow knows she's spending too much money, Grant calls. Startled by the vibration in her jean pocket, she pulls out her phone and frowns.

"What's wrong?" she asks, panic settling in her voice.

"Nothing's wrong," whispers Grant.

"Then why are you whispering?" Darby types in her address for the delivery.

"I wanted to check on you."

"I'm fine! Really." Darby opens the delivery link for Whole Foods and browses through the week's specials.

"Good. So listen, I was thinking I would surprise Camille by flying her parents out here in a few weeks. Maybe have a small baby shower?"

"Oh, Grant, that's so sweet." She clicks on a case of seltzer water flavored with lime and adds it to her order. "But hey, how about you let me plan the actual shower?"

"Would you really want to do that?"

"It's the least I could do." Darby opens her calendar on her laptop and asks, "What day were you thinking?"

"I was hoping we could do it on the fourteenth."

"Valentine's Day?" She adds an assortment of microwaveable frozen vegetables and a couple of vegetarian frozen burritos to the order. "Not like I have plans or anything. Hey, what's that oatmeal stuff you're always eating?"

"Kashi. Are you really okay with planning the details for the shower? Camille doesn't like a big spectacle."

"I'll make sure it's not over the top." Darby pays for her online Whole Foods order and then opens Pinterest. "Shit," she mumbles.

"What?" Grant asks.

"I left whisky bottles in the hall and someone's knocking on my door. I'll call you back." Hanging up with Grant, Darby stands from her desk and searches for another top from her dresser. She grabs a navy tank top with a bleach stain, puts it on backwards, and the heads to the door.

"I'm coming," she shouts in response to another knock. Moving the trash bags away from the door so she can unlatch the chain, she mentally practices what she'll say to the old bitty waiting to report her to the building. *I'm donating them to a charity auction for a carnival game,* she rehearses.

But as Darby opens the door to deliver an Emmy-award-winning monologue about the boxes of bottles, she doesn't find the old bitty who hates her. Instead, leaning against the door-frame with a smile that's equal parts sexy and charming, is Darby's leading man.

Her mouth drops open and she gasps, and if it weren't for the bags of garbage pressing against her legs and holding her upright, she'd probably fall over as well.

Anthony reaches out for her and then stops, his smile fading to a frown as he notices the sutured gash on her head, glistening with sweat. "What happened?"

"You're here," she whispers, her voice sounding tiny in comparison to his loud boom.

"Of course I'm here." He takes a step forward and squeezes past the door.

Making room, Darby takes a step backward but loses her balance. Anthony comes to her rescue and swoops her in his arms like a paper doll. He steps over the mound of garbage bags and then sets her down inside the apartment.

Breathless, she utters, "Hey."

He smiles, noting the change in the color of her eyes. "Hi." Anthony slides his hand behind her head and tenderly kisses her wound. He trails his lips over her bruised cheek, and then stops at her mouth. He hovers just close enough to tease Darby with his breath.

And then, parting her lips with his tongue, Anthony delivers on his promise.

Chapter Thirteen

Once the garage to a firehouse, the dilapidated aluminum siding and concrete slab now serve as Anthony's workshop. Wanting more natural lighting, he raises the paneled garage door halfway, and then flips on the power to a small space heater.

Getting down on one knee, he installs a safety track to the drawer of a bedside table. He then runs a small piece of tack cloth over the thin legs and inside the cubbyhole. Removing the original knob from his shirt pocket, Anthony attaches it to the drawer and gives it a try. "Perfect," he says, standing from the cement floor to admire his work. "Now, how in the hell am I getting you to Tribeca?"

Turning off the space heater, Anthony checks the time on the clock radio, and then folds a plastic tarp. He closes the garage door and locks it from inside, pulls the chain to the naked lightbulb, and then heads out the side door. Shivering in his flannel jacket, he jogs the three blocks back to his apartment.

When he reaches his modest duplex off of Bell Avenue, Anthony kicks the snow off of his boots and checks the mailbox. Unlocking the door that leads to the kitchen, he grabs a beer from the refrigerator as his cousin, Joey, waltzes into the kitchen wearing a suit and tie.

"You finally took a job as a car salesman?" teases Anthony, twisting off the cap to his beer.

Joey adjusts his tie and says, "I'm taking Gina out for Valentine's Day."

"Valentine's Day was five days ago."

"She had to work. Besides, everybody knows that restaurants raise their prices on V-day."

"You make a point." Anthony leans against the counter and drinks his beer. "So, hey, can I borrow your car tonight?"

"Are you deaf? I just said I'm taking Gina out for dinner."

"Use her car."

"You didn't really think that motorcycle purchase all the way through, huh?"

"Psshh, you're crazy. My '65 Yamaha is fucking sweet." He lets out a desperate sigh and asks, "Can I borrow your car or not?"

"What's in it for me?"

"What do you want?"

Joey cocks a brow and scratches his chin. "Two hundred should do it."

Crossing his arms, Anthony shakes his head. "I can rent a car for forty."

"Let's make it fifty."

"I get the Mazda for the night?" confirms Anthony, pulling out his wallet and removing a fifty.

Joey snatches the cash from his cousin's hand and passes him a set of keys with a keychain of a corno horn. "Just don't mess with my sound system, okay? I know how you love *The Cure*."

"Funny," replies Anthony.

"Oh, and bring Darby to dinner with the family next week." Joey points to the ceiling and chortles. "Nonno was asking about *la bella rossa*."

"I'm workin' on it." Anthony sets the keys on the counter and then punches Joey's arm. "Have fun tonight."

Leaving his dopey cousin in the kitchen, Anthony runs up the stairs and hurries to his bedroom. He rips off his clothes and drops them to the floor, quietly opening the door to the bathroom. Listening to her sing show tunes, he slides the shower curtain to the side and steps in the tub. Sneaking up behind her, he kisses her shoulder and pokes her with his hard erection.

"Ack!" Darby shrieks, turning to face her intruder. "Did you finish the table?"

"Yep." Using his large frame to block the water, he instructs Darby to turn back around. "Face the wall and spread your legs." He glides his hand between her soapy legs and gently pries them apart.

"Oh, wow," she moans, as Anthony rubs his cock against her ass.

"You're so wet," he whispers into her ear.

"Literally," they say in unison.

Arching her back, Darby reaches behind and glides her hand over the smooth skin of his shaft. "Are you sure we have time for this?"

Anthony bites her neck, aroused by the way his mouth marks her body. "We'll always have time for this."

Carrying the large box Darby insisted on using, Anthony leans against the back wall of the elevator and asks, "Does your brother like football?"

Darby shrugs her shoulders. "Maybe. He ran cross country and threw those spear thingies in high school."

"Javelin," he mumbles.

"Hey, just relax and be yourself."

"He's your brother."

"Yeah, but trust me, you'll intimidate *him*."

"I want them to like me, Darby."

As the elevator doors open, she pinches his ass. "What's not to like?"

Taking a deep breath, Anthony adjusts the box in his arms while Darby knocks on the door.

"Oh, my, God!" She presses a button under the brass apartment numbers. "Two years and I never saw this buzzer."

Opening the door in her black wig, black tank top, and black leggings, Camille beams with excitement. "Darby! Anthony! Get in here."

Hearing the noise at the door, Grant comes barreling in with a glass of scotch and his hand out ready for a handshake.

"Jesus Christ, Grant." Darby frowns at his brown cashmere sweater and then flicks his arm. "Let's not make this formal, Mr. Cleaver."

Setting the box on the floor, Anthony extends his hand. "Hey, I'm Anthony Napolitano. This is a great apartment."

"Let me take your coats," says Camille, giving Darby the secret girl nod of approval.

"We can't stay long." Darby wraps her arms around Anthony's waist and smiles. "But we wanted to drop off your surprise."

"Ooh, what is it?" Camille asks.

Darby gently kicks the box with her foot and says, "Grant, be a good lad and take it to the nursery, will ya?"

Grant hands his drink to Camille and then bends over to pick up the box.

Watching him struggle with the bulk, Darby teases, "Almost there, big boy!"

"You're so mean," whispers Anthony, nudging her side.

As they follow Grant to the nursery, Camille taps on Darby's shoulder and asks, "How did the doctor go?"

"He gave me some sort of wonder cream." She pulls back her hair to reveal the silky scar. "Sixty bucks a tube, but totally worth it."

"Oh, yeah. You look great!" Camille checks out Anthony's ass as she drops Grant's drink off in the kitchen.

Inside the nursery, Anthony helps Grant lift the table out of the box. They position it next to a modern rocking chair, and then Grant sets a small lamp on the top.

"Where are your parents, Camille?" asks Darby, picking up a tiny pair of booties from the dresser and making them tap dance in air.

Rubbing her belly as she waddles into the nursery, she replies, "Oh, Dad had to return to San Fran for work, and Mom had tickets to *The Color Purple*."

Stepping aside to reveal the surprise, Anthony announces, "Ta da!"

Camille lunges toward Anthony and hugs him. "Holy crap! Did you restore this yourself?"

Humbled, he nods with a smile.

"Well, it's the perfect addition to the room!"

"It's pretty amazing." Grant opens the little drawer and the closes it. "Is this walnut?"

"Yeah, and it was in great shape." Anthony leans against a tall dresser and crosses his arms. "The drawer pull is original to the piece, so all I had to do was clean it up and let the wood shine."

Camille sits in the rocker and switches on the lamp. "Thank you, both," she says, as Bogart strolls into the nursery to investigate.

"Hey, kitty." Anthony squats down to scratch his head. "You're so fat and happy."

"Aw, he likes you," jokes Darby.

Hearing the oven timer go off, Camille pulls herself up from the rocker and shuffles to the door. "I think the vegetarian lasagna is done."

Grant follows her out of the nursery while glancing back at Darby and Anthony. "Don't eat it," he mouths.

"So we should probably get going." Anthony stands and nudges the cat with his foot. "Is he dead?"

"Nah, he's just summoning his inner Garfield." Darby removes a blue box with a white ribbon from her purse. She places it on the dresser next to the baby booties, and then, with a sigh of utter happiness, she takes Anthony's hand. "C'mon, let's get out of here before we're forced to eat vegetables."

"Hey, you promised to show me the Gotham office."

"Okay, but let me do the talking and you just keep walking," she orders, pulling him through the living room to avoid the kitchen. "Camille, we have reservations in twenty minutes." Darby yanks

Anthony's hand and then opens the door to the apartment. "I'll see you Monday for our yoga class."

"You take yoga?" whispers Anthony.

"No, of course not. It's code for shopping." She closes the door and furrows her brows. "What's wrong?"

"You didn't even let me say good-bye. They'll think I'm rude."

"If it means that much to you," she opens the door, "then tell them now."

Pinching Darby's side, Anthony shouts, "Bye – it was nice meeting you." He shuts the door and laughs. "You're gonna get it, Shortcake!"

"Mmm, are you going to spank me?" Darby shakes her ass as she unlocks the door to the office. "Welcome to our media hub." She flips on the light in the reception area and then leads Anthony to her desk. "As you can see, I have a window office."

"And a lot of fan mail." Anthony picks up a stack of mail and flips through the envelopes. "Here's a good one from the Fulton Correctional Facility."

She clicks her tongue and reaches for the stack of mail. "Give me that." But as she opens a drawer to dump the mail, a crisp, linen envelope falls to the floor. Noticing a peacock feather embossed on the back seal, she quickly bends down to recover it. "Lucas?" she mutters.

"Who?"

Intrigued, she rips open the envelope and carefully slides out an invitation. "Lucas is this guy I met . . . he was doing research . . . or he wrote a book – I can't remember."

"The people of New Amsterdam," Anthony reads aloud.

Darby pins the invitation to her schedule board and says, "You should come with me."

"To a lecture?"

"It could be fun!"

"Fine." He sits down in the desk chair and grabs her hips. "Hop on."

"Hop on what exactly?"

He pats his upper thighs and waggles his brows.

NEW YORK LECTURE SERIES

PRESENTED BY THE AMERICAN HISTORICAL ASSOCIATION

THE TROYER STEELE ANDERSON NOMINEE

DR. LUCAS PHILLIPS

THE PEOPLE OF NEW AMSTERDAM

March 12, 2016 at 7pm
National Museum of the American Indian
1 Bowling Green, New York, NY 10004

RSVP to barbaraclark@nyu.edu

Darby sits on his lap and leans back against his chest. "This chair spins."

"Oh yeah?" He kicks his foot against the floor and turns the chair to make a full rotation.

"Faster!" she orders, crisscrossing her legs.

Anthony spins the chair until Darby makes him stop, and when they stop, he angles their position so that they can admire the twinkling lights of the West Side skyline.

"Are you dizzy?"

Darby glances at their reflection in the window and grins. "Yeah, like I'm falling."

"Twelve long months, hundreds of strangers, ten leather journals, and three thousand pages of research, have led me to one conclusion – love can only be defined by the people of New Amsterdam."

Chapter Fourteen

Rubbing her eyes, Darby emails the latest post for Gotham Online to Grant, and then closes her laptop. She stands from the desk chair and stretches her arms behind her back, watching as an afternoon downpour smacks against the window. "I think we'll need a boat if we want to get to Queens."

With a lazy smile, Anthony throws back the duvet and slaps Darby's pillow. "Come back to bed."

"But we have plans with your family." Without hesitating, Darby pulls off her sweatpants and crawls into the bed next to him. Trailing her finger over his hairy chest, she then draws invisible hearts across his hard stomach. "I love that you sleep in the nude."

Guiding her hand toward his erection, Anthony closes his eyes when she strokes his shaft. "What were you working on?"

"A Gotham post I titled, *A Farewell to February*." She runs her palm over the tip of his cock and says, "And since today is the last day of the month, I need to get it up tonight."

"Nope," he groans.

"No, what? You don't like this?" she asks, loosening her grasp around the head.

"Oh, I like that." Anthony slides his finger under the spaghetti strap of Darby's tank and pulls it off her shoulder. "It's a Leap Year."

With her hand cupping his balls, and her pinky finger massaging the perineum, she growls, "Sonovabitch."

Anthony opens his eyes and turns to face her, laughing at her aversion to the month of February. "It's not that big of a deal." He kisses her pouty frown and tickles her side.

"But I want it to be March! I want spring, and tulips, and the chance to wear cute shoes."

"True, but I was thinking about how . . ."

Darby's phone vibrates underneath her pillow. She ignores it, but then it buzzes again. "Hold that thought." Placing a finger over Anthony's lips, she reads a text.

Grant: Camille's water broke – on the way to the hospital.

"Camille's having the baby!"

Leaping from the bed, Anthony pulls on his boxer briefs and peeks over Darby's shoulder. "Like right now?" he asks, reading the text exchange.

Darby: Should I come now?

Grant: No, I'll text when she's further along. Oh, and she insists on wearing that wig.

"What wig?" asks Anthony, searching for his phone somewhere on the desk.

"The black wig she was wearing when you met her."

"That was a wig?"

"Long story – which ironically involves you – but yeah." Darby gets out of the bed and straightens the sheets and fluffs the pillows. "Camille has long, sun-kissed surfer hair."

Shaking his head in disbelief, Anthony dials his parents' phone number. "Nonno, it's me, Antonio. Can you put Mama on the phone?"

"Will they be upset if we cancel dinner?" whispers Darby.

"Nah, they just really want to meet you." On hold, because Nonno still hasn't mastered the magic of cordless phones, Anthony draws a smiley face on the damp window above the radiator.

"I'm hopping in the shower," Darby says as she heads to the

bathroom. She starts the shower and then glances at her forehead in the mirror. Taking a closer look, she runs a finger over the silky scar – a subtle reminder that she's a work in progress. Darby removes her underwear and tank, and then steps into the shower and closes the glass door.

Joining her in the bathroom, Anthony leans against the sink and crosses his arms. "Darby?"

"Everything okay?" she asks, rinsing shampoo from her hair.

"Oh, yeah. My mom wants me to take a box of rainbow cookies over to Camille." He scratches the stubble on his chin and says, "So I was thinking earlier . . . do you believe in fate?"

Applying conditioner to her ends, she utters, "Um, I believe in karma."

"Okay, so the way we met, what do you call that?"

Thinking back to her conversation with Lucas all those weeks ago, Darby looks up at the ceiling and laughs. "Oh, my, God!"

"What's so funny?"

Turning to face him, she draws a heart on the glass shower door. "Beefcake, we had a meet-cute."

Several blocks east, on the other side of Battery Park, one of New York's finest examples of Beaux-Arts architecture can be found at the Alexander Hamilton U.S. Custom House. A City landmark, the building also serves as the Smithsonian National Museum of the American Indian – which is the perfect venue for a prominent historian of indigenous people to kick off his lecture tour.

Completing a final walk-through of the space, Dr. Lucas Phillips stands behind a podium and whistles. "Pretty impressive, Barbara," he says, turning to his secretary.

"The AHA is very excited to host the lecture series." She pushes her glasses up the narrow bridge of her nose and continues. "So after the Q and A, we'll move to the adjoining room for cocktails. Any special requests?"

Lucas rubs the back of his neck and laughs. "New Amsterdam vodka, of course."

"No, seriously."

"Just keep it simple, Barbara."

Taking notes as they descend the steps of the stage, she says, "I'll ask the vendor we use for university parties."

"Great idea." He gently grabs her arm and pulls her in the other direction. "I want to show you something." Lucas guides Barbara toward a display of authentic headdresses and headbands. "Do you see that one?" He taps on the glass and points to a modest Lenape headband fashioned with beaded deerskin and a single feather. "The one behind the roach headdress."

"Wow, is that a peacock feather?"

"A peacock feather is a strange choice for a Lenape Indian, don't you think?"

Barbara shrugs her shoulders. "Dr. Phillips, you're the expert."

Laughing, he places his hand on her shoulder and leads her back to the Custom House. "Do you have a current RSVP list?" he asks, admiring the rotunda of the lobby.

She removes a spreadsheet from her binder and says, "Here's a printout from this morning." Stopping at the coat check, Barbara hands the attendant a ticket for their coats and umbrellas. "I hope the rain stops."

"Yeah, me too," he mumbles, focused on the four pages of names.

Lucas walks to a bench and sits down, flipping back to the beginning of the list. He smiles when he sees the names, Thessaly Sinclair, Julia Pierce, and Darby Wallace – all three noting a plus one on their RSVP.

"Here's your coat, Dr. Phillips." Barbara hands him his twill commuter jacket and then asks, "Everything okay?"

Glancing up from the spreadsheet, he frowns. "She hasn't replied."

Lowering her voice, Barbara assures, "Well, no, not yet. But we still have two weeks."

"And you're sure she got the invitation?"

"I used certified mail like you asked."

Standing from the bench and folding the spreadsheet, Lucas puts on his coat and takes his umbrella. "Okay. Let me walk you out."

As they leave the museum, Barbara thanks her contact in the administration office. "Dr. Phillips, you can go ahead. I need to go over the staffing details with Helen."

"I can wait," he offers.

"No need."

"Okay then," he says, quickly pecking her on the cheek. "Have a great weekend, Barbara."

Lucas steps outside the main entrance to the Custom House and opens his NYU umbrella, a gift from the faculty Christmas party. The streets are empty, and there are no cabs to be seen, so hurrying to the nearest corner, he stops under protective scaffolding and taps his foot. Left or right . . . north or west . . .

Go to her, he tells himself.

He heads north on Broadway, walking under the makeshift canopy as long as he can, and then jogging in his leather wingtips the last few blocks to Fulton Street. Lucas stops at the crosswalk and catches his breath, debating his next move.

And then he sees her, shivering in the rain as she waits outside her building. Her hair is longer, and her coat is new, but to Lucas, she's his first and only love.

He wants to yell out to her, and he wants to take her in his arms and make everything right. But as Lucas crosses the street, a blue Lexus GS F screeches to a stop in front of her. She happily bounces into the street, walks in front of the car, and then closes her red umbrella as she slides into the passenger's seat.

"Wait," he shouts, approaching the car.

The rain is heavy, and Lucas can't see her face, but the man behind the wheel, egotistical bastard that he is, glances at Lucas with a smug grin. And then the Lexus speeds off, aiming the front tire at a sloshy puddle where the street meets the curb. Dirty water violently spatters on the sidewalk, drenching Lucas' pants, and ruining his expensive shoes.

Lucas clenches the handle of his umbrella while focusing on the car's bumper. He memorizes the license plate number . . . which will eventually be traced to New Amsterdam's resident douchebag – the sexist, homophobic, racist motherfucker, Paul Holbrook.

Damn, that guy really has it coming.

Italian-American Dictionary

aduzipach!/aduzipazz! – you're crazy! (*ma tu sei pazzo!*) [aa-DOO-zee-PAACH]/[aa-DOO-zee-PAATS]

afanabola!/vafanabola!/a fa napule! – go to hell! (*a fa Napoli!*) [aa-faa-NAA-boe-laa]

ammonini! – let's go! (*andiamo!*) [aa-moe-NEE-nee]

boombots – nickname for an idiot (*u' pazzo*); Note: As in "Vinnie Boombots" [boom-BAATS]

buttagots/butta' gazz' – annoying idiot (*buttana u' cazzo*) [boo-taa-GAATS]

chooch – jackass (*ciuccio*) [CHOOCH]

facciu fridda – it's cold (*fa freddo*) [FAA-choo-FREE-daa]

'ffangul'! – go fuck yourself! (*vai a fare in culo*) – [faan-GOOL]

gabbaruss'/gab' a' russ' – redhead (*capo rosso*) [gaa-baa-ROOS]

gabish?/capish?/gabisc'? – (do you) understand? (*capisci?*) [gaa-PEESH]

gavone – gluttonous eater (*cafone*) [gaa-VOAN]

ghiacchieron' – blabbermouth (*chiacchierone*) [gyaa-kyaa-ROAN]

goombah – countryman/fellow comrade/godfather (*compare*) [goom-BAA]

manigott' – italian pasta (*manicotti*) [maa-NEE-gauwt]

oobatz'/patz' – crazy person (*un pazzo/u' pazzu*) [oo-BAATZ]

paesan' – fellow Italian countryman (*paesano*) [pai-ZAAN]

scustumad' – stupid person (*scostumato*) [skoo-stoo-MAAD]

statagitt'!/stagitt'!/staizitt'!/staizii! –*be quiet!* (*stai zitto*) [stah-tuh-JEET]

stunad – moron (*stonato*) [stoo-NAAD]

ue, goombah! – hey, man! (*ue, compare!*) [way-goom-BAH]

vaffangul'!/baffangul'!/ – fuck you! (*vai a fare in culo*) [VAA-faan-GOOL]

Darby Playlist

While I Shovel the Snow	The Walkmen
Boys Don't Cry	The Cure
Whiskey River	Willie Nelson
Don't Forget Me	The Head and the Heart
Where is my Mind?	Pixies
Winter Winds	Mumford & Sons
White Winter Hymnal	Fleet Foxes
Winter in my Heart	The Avett Brothers
Cold, Cold Heart	Norah Jones
Moon River	Audrey Hepburn
All We Ever Knew	The Head and the Heart

Merci Beaucoup!

With gratitude and appreciation, I'd like to acknowledge the following:

Vincent Pullo

Erika Q. Stokes

Molly Van Roekel

Marla Esposito

Nick Fantini

Christina Mock

Brenna Rattai

Jamie Beshears

Les Femmes

The Indie community

Mom & Dad

Luke & Sydney

Roscoe & Zoe

New York City

DSNY

Netflix

Groundhog Day directed by Harold Ramis

Rachel's Holiday written by Marian Keyes

Let's Be Still album by the Head and the Heart

Sonic Highways television series documented by Dave Grohl

Humans of New York created and photographed by Brandon Stanton

And you.

About the Author

Residing in New York with her husband and two children, Ashley Pullo is an author, an entertainment blogger, and an advocate for cultural literacy.

Hey y'all!

NYC is an amazing place to find inspiration - the random and the ordinary that make up reality. My writing showcases inspired ideas, as well as my love for dichotomy, authenticity, pop-culture, and humor.

Dreams need chasers.

Facebook www.facebook.com/AshleyPullo
Twitter @ashpullo
Instagram @apauthor
MY AMAZING WEBSITE http://www.ashleypullo.com

Find me at my local Starbucks around 3 p.m.

Other Works by Ashley Pullo

Discography Series:

The Album

The Ballad

The Love Letters

New Amsterdam Series:

Tess

Julia